Nantucket
RED

Nantucket RED

LEILA HOWLAND

HYPERION
LOS ANGELES · NEW YORK

First Edition
1 3 5 7 9 10 8 6 4 2
G475-5664-5-14046

Printed in the United States of America

Library of Congress Cataloging-in-Publication Data
Howland, Leila.
Nantucket red/Leila Howland.—First edition.
pages cm
Sequel to: Nantucket blue.
Summary: "Before starting college, Cricket Thompson returns to
Nantucket for a summer filled with hard choices and infinite possibility"
—Provided by publisher.
ISBN 978-1-4231-6095-3 (hardback)—ISBN 1-4231-6095-9
[1. Dating (Social customs)—Fiction. 2. Love—Fiction. 3. Summer
employment—Fiction. 4. Nantucket Island (Mass.)—Fiction.] I. Title.
PZ7.H8465Nc 2014
[Fic]—dc23   2013049036

Reinforced binding

Visit www.hyperionteens.com

SUSTAINABLE FORESTRY INITIATIVE   Certified Sourcing
www.sfiprogram.org
SFI-00993

THIS LABEL APPLIES TO TEXT STOCK

For Jonathan

One

I NEVER LIKED THE LAST FEW DAYS OF SUMMER VACATION. Hot without the promise of beach days, heavy with the knowledge that a whole school year is ahead, and stuck in a muggy haze between summer and fall, they're the slowest days of the year. Today felt like the most in-between day of all. It was almost eleven o'clock and I was still in bed. The sun streaked through the blinds and made patterns on the walls. I stared at the ceiling, watching the fan go around and around. Zack was starting boarding school tomorrow and we still hadn't discussed whether we were going to stay together or break up. How was it that only a week ago we were at Steps Beach, kissing under the stars, with what felt like an ocean of time sparkling ahead of us?

A few days after we'd returned to Providence, Zack told

me he was going to Hanover Academy, an elite boarding school in northern New Hampshire. I understood why he was leaving. His mom, Nina, had died in June and his dad and sister, Jules, had completely shut down. Who could blame them?

Nina was the most alive person I'd ever met. I loved her, too. She taught me how to ice skate backward. She taught me how to make a perfect vinaigrette. She introduced me to Frida Kahlo and William Carlos Williams. She made the best paella. There was no one like her, and now she was gone. Mr. Clayton and Jules were shadows of their previous selves. Zack was living with ghosts.

Hanover would give him a chance to start fresh and be among the living. When he told me that a space had opened up at the last minute and he was taking it, I was happy for him. It didn't feel real. I still had Nantucket sand in my shoes. I was so dizzy-happy in love with him that nothing felt real, but it was starting to sink in: the boy I'd risked everything for this summer was going away. He was coming over in a few hours to spend the afternoon with me, and we had to decide what to do. Break up? I wondered as I kicked off the sheets. Stay together, I thought, and sat up.

I lifted my hair off my sweaty neck, twisted it into a bun, and turned on my laptop. When I logged onto Facebook, Zack's new profile picture was at the top of my feed. He'd taken down the photo of himself on the beach in Nantucket and replaced it with one of himself in a Hanover Academy sweatshirt. No, I thought.

Jules commented: "Don't forget your jockstrap!"

A flurry of "good lucks" and "have funs" and more specific comments followed, references to Hanover that I didn't
understand. No, stay with me, I thought and felt myself contract and stiffen. My jaw tightened. My stomach clenched.
I wanted to hold on to him and keep him in my world, our
world. This feeling, this panicky collapse, was opposite of
the sweet effervescence I felt when I was with him; it was
foreign and unwelcome, and it didn't feel like love.

"Cricket, it's for you," Mom said with a girlie smile when
Zack knocked on the door a few hours later. Mom had
never been good with boundaries; my being in love gave her
a contact blush.

Zack's eyes lit up as I walked toward him in the new
white tank top Mom had bought me from the Gap after
she saw the state of my clothes when I'd returned from
Nantucket, and my old, worn-out cutoffs she couldn't have
separated me from if she'd tried. My hair was still damp
from a shower and I knew I smelled like the vanilla soap he
liked. A slow grin spread across his face as he leaned in the
door frame.

"Let's get lost," Zack said like someone from an old
movie. He handed me an iced coffee just the way I liked it:
extra ice, lots of cream, no sugar.

Mom lingered in the front hall and placed a hand over
her heart, slayed by Zack's charm. "Don't forget to take an
umbrella," she said. "It's supposed to rain."

"That's okay. Thanks, Mom," I said as we walked to his car. I slid my fingers through his belt loop. "I know where we can get some privacy." I'd discovered this place on an away game in Newport. It was about a half hour outside Providence, off Route 24, past Dotty's Donuts, down a shady country road. You had to drive by the farm with the self-service strawberry stand and the Catholic school with its low, humble buildings, all the way to where the road ended at the Narragansett Bay.

The air-conditioning was broken in Zack's old station wagon, so we drove with the windows down. We listened to the college station, stopped for donuts, and even spotted one of the monks from the Catholic school talking on an iPhone. We held hands and kissed at stoplights, but we didn't talk about us.

After we parked, Zack headed down to the beach. I balanced on the abandoned train tracks that hugged the shore and watched him pick up a stone, examine it, and send it skipping into the bay. He was having dinner with Jules and his dad in an hour and a half, and then they were heading to New Hampshire, where they would spend the night at an inn so they could move him into his dorm the next morning. It was time.

I hopped off the tracks, walked down the rocky hill to the beach, and wrapped my arms around his waist. There was a pale band on his neck where his hair had been cut for school.

"What are we going to do?" I asked, breathing into his back.

"I don't want to break up," he said, turning to face me. The clouds collected weight and darkness above us. He pulled me close. "What do you think?"

"I think long distance sucks." Zack pressed his fingers into my spine, confusing my chemicals. Part of me was trying to shut down so that I could deal with this, but my blood spun under his touch.

"It's only a few hours away. We can switch off weekends."

"I don't have a car."

"You can take the bus. And there are so many vacations. For as expensive as this school is, I'll hardly ever be there."

"But I don't want to be someone you text or a face on the screen," I said as his hands left swirls of heat on my back. "We'll forget each other. Or fade away. Long distance will distort everything."

"I could never forget you," Zack said as a wave washed over our ankles. My shoes got soaked. I tossed them back on the beach where they landed in ballet third position.

"When I saw you'd changed your profile picture, I felt like this." I clenched my fists and gritted my teeth. He smiled. "Zack, I'm serious." I looped my arms around his neck and leaned in. "I don't want to feel that way about you. All tight and anxious."

"Let's not do long distance, then."

"So we're breaking up?" The words were so far from

what I wanted that they didn't feel real—like I couldn't have possibly just said them. "No, no, no. I don't want that."

"I don't either."

"Maybe we can just . . . pause," I said.

"What do you mean?"

"I mean, we'll just stop here, right now, like this, and then pick up where we left off next summer." A few fat raindrops fell. "No Facebook, no Instagram, no texts, no phone."

"Okay," Zack said. "I can do that."

"But we have to stick to the rules, otherwise the pause won't work."

"I'm unfriending you right now." Zack slid one hand in my left back pocket while the other took out his phone. "Well, there's no reception out here, but I'm going to do it as soon as I get home." Then, before I knew it, Zack snapped a picture of us: me looking up as the rain started, eyebrows raised, him with his arm around my neck, smiling at me.

The rain started for real. We ran for the car and dove into the backseat. Rain splattered against the windows as if flung from a million paintbrushes.

"Paused," I said.

"Paused," Zack said. He pulled off my tank top and I slid his T-shirt over his head.

"Wait—the monk!" I said, covering myself with my hands.

"He's on his iPhone," Zack said, and we laughed, trying to guess who it was he was talking to: His mom? A nun? God?

"I love you," he said as we slid back on the seat.

"I love you, too." It was the first time we'd said those three words in that order. I shivered. I knew in my bones that the words were as true and real as the vinyl seats in that wood-paneled station wagon, the rusted rails of the train tracks, the drumroll of thunder in the distance. My foot made a print on the cool, fogged-up window.

Forty-five minutes later, flushed and unable to stop smiling, we drove off. I'd forgotten all about my shoes, which had been left on the beach, waiting, in third position, for our return.

Two

FOR THE FIRST TIME IN MY THIRTEEN YEARS OF ATTENDING the Rosewood School for Girls, I was scared to walk through the front doors. I should've been happy. As a senior, I was going to be allowed off campus for lunch. I was going to write the name of whatever colleges I was accepted into on the big piece of butcher paper hanging in the senior lounge. I was going to be captain of the field hockey and lacrosse teams, and for years I'd planned on being one of the seniors who was super nice to the freshman. As I watched girls spill out of cars in spanking-new uniforms, and gather in quartets and trios, I didn't feel nice.

"I can't go in," I said to Mom. "Jules hates me."

"She doesn't hate you. She's been through hell, but you did nothing wrong."

"What about Nina's memorial service?" I leaned against the headrest to offset the nausea.

"You thought you were doing the right thing. It was an innocent mistake."

"Zack?" *Innocent* was not the word to describe us.

"Falling in love with someone's brother is not a hanging offense," Mom said and checked herself out in the visor mirror. She applied a new shade of lipstick. Coral. It was actually kind of hip. She'd been taking antidepressants for three weeks now and I could tell they were starting to work. She readjusted the mirror. "Now, out you go, I can't be late. It's my first day, too, you know."

I shook my head. God only knows how Jules had spun the story of this summer to our friends. She could tell a story like no one else: pauses so well timed, impressions so accurate, gestures so precise that everyone in her orbit was enchanted. My stomach churned at the thought of being on the wrong side of her talent.

Mom leaned over and opened the door herself. "Cricket, go."

I was biding my time in a bathroom stall before assembly, admiring the paint job they'd done over the summer, when Jules came in. I watched her walk into the next stall. I would know those boat shoes anywhere, as well as the little white scar on the top of her left foot from when she'd dropped an ice skate in the seventh grade. The sound of her peeing seemed horribly amplified. She was humming the school song. I was going to make a run for it, but then I realized that catching her alone was exactly what I needed. I had to face her and apologize again. Better that we weren't surrounded. I opened the latch, stood by the sinks, and braced myself.

"I'm sorry," I said, when she emerged from the stall.

"Ah!" She flung a hand to her chest. "You scared me."

"I'm sorry. About the memorial service, and Zack, and everything."

"Cricket." Jules sighed my name. She looked tired, a little too tan, a little too skinny. I wanted to hug her and ask if she was okay. "I just— I can't right now." She'd said it with such naked honesty there was nothing to do but accept it.

"Okay," I said. "Okay." We washed our hands in silence. We couldn't walk out together. In a strange move, I gestured like some kind of old-fashioned gentleman for her to leave first. She gave me a confused look and left. I counted to twenty and opened the door. I saw our group of friends seamlessly envelop her as they walked toward assembly, moving in one fluid motion, like a river.

They'd repainted the auditorium, too, and even though the windows were open, the fumes were giving me a headache. I sat up front, away from Jules, and tried to focus as the principal, Edwina MacIntosh, welcomed everyone back to school. Teachers made announcements about school activities: student council, the literary magazine, yearbook, choir, community service outreach. Sign me up for everything, I thought. I may be without a best friend or a boyfriend, but this is my school.

I cast a quick glance at Jules, who was whispering to Arti Rai. My college application is going to fucking glow, I thought as I whipped out my plan book and started making notes.

I spent the midmorning break alone in the senior lounge with my school supplies. I could see Jules in the cafeteria, telling summer stories to a table of enraptured girls. They were all eating bagels the way I had invented, peeling off the hard outer shell and eating that first and saving the squishy middle in its original shape for last. That's called Cricket-style, I thought bitterly. I was eating an endlessly chewy protein bar that tasted like wood chips, labeling tabs, and trying to look busy. Miss Kang, the field hockey and lacrosse coach, noticed me as she walked by.

I smiled and held up my plan book. "Getting organized!"

"You are too much, Cricket," she said and sat down next to me on the old couch. "You know I'm in touch with Stacy, head coach over at Brown, right? She's got her eye on you. What do you say we put together some clips to send her?" She elbowed me. "What do you say we get you into Brown?"

"Really? Do you think?" I'd always imagined I'd go away for college and not stay in Providence. Where, I didn't know, but I had this picture in my head of stuffing the Honda to the gills and hitting the road. But Brown was *Ivy League*— hallowed words, a synonym for the best. I imagined what it would feel like to write *Brown* on that big piece of butcher paper. It would feel like redemption. I'd seen it happen. The senior girls accepted to Ivy Leagues basked in a haze of adoration, cleansed of all previous misdeeds. "Do you really think I could make the team?"

"They'd be lucky to have you," Miss Kang said. "And they're going to graduate their starting lineup this year." She rubbed her hands together as if devising a plan. Then, glimpsing the clock in the cafeteria, she said, "I have to prep for Algebra II. We'll talk more at practice. You should be ready to lead warm-ups with Jules."

"Yeah, sure." Cocaptains. It had been decided last year, back when we could bust into our synchronized dance moves within three seconds of hearing that Bruno Mars song, but now my stomach elevator-dropped at her name. "No problem."

Three

IT WAS ALMOST HALFTIME AND PEABODY SCHOOL WAS
beating us three to zero. The field hockey season was not
off to a good start. We'd won only one game out of four,
and that was against Hamlin. Everyone could beat Hamlin.
But this game was embarrassing. They were playing their
second string in the first half. I think they were even giving
some of their JV players a shot. And it was the first cold day
of the year. We'd gone from summer to winter in a week
with only one crisp, sweater-weather day in between. Out
on Peabody's field, it was overcast and the air had teeth.

The ref blew the whistle in our favor for the first time
the whole game. Jules had the ball. She tapped her elbow.
That meant she'd hit the ball hard and long up the field,
which was my cue to sprint, make it look like I was going to

shoot, and then pass it back to Jules, who would hopefully score. But instead of wielding her stick like an ax, thwacking the ball and sending it flying, she tapped it. It rolled ten feet.

I darted for the ball, hooked it, and started dribbling. My eyes were on the goal, but my head was elsewhere. I knew there was a Halloween party that weekend at Jay Logan's and that a bunch of girls were getting ready at Jules's house. They'd talked about it right in front of me on the bus while I'd pretended to be fascinated by the highway scenery. I was tired of sitting out social events because of Jules. I'd done my time. I wanted to go out and have fun. But what was I going to do, show up alone? Invite myself over to her house to get ready?

"Cricket," Jules called, but I charged ahead, weaving through Peabody's line of defense. I was about to take a shot when a Peabody player, a freshman, I think, stole the ball right out from under me. How did I not see her? The buzzer sounded.

"That's half!" the ref called.

"Cricket and Jules, get over here," Miss Kang said. Her face was red with cold or anger or both. She gestured with a blunt-nailed index finger. "You two need to get it together. You're the captains. You need to be communicating. You're on different planets out there. What the hell is going on?"

I looked at Jules. She shrugged and stared at the ground. Her breath formed faint clouds in front of her perfect, heart-shaped lips.

"Um? You know what?" Miss Kang lowered her voice and looked over her shoulder. Our teammates looked on in curiosity. "Whatever drama you two are going through is taking down the team, and it sucks. You need to decide if you're up to this. If you're not, we need new captains. It's not fair to the other girls. You have five minutes to work this out or I'm holding an emergency election."

Miss Kang marched off. I took in a lungful of frosty air. If we quit it would look terrible on my applications. I was not going to let Jules mar my résumé.

"Well?" I said. Jules wouldn't look at me. "Ugh!" I threw down my stick. "Enough is enough! I apologized on Nantucket. I apologized the first day of school. I feel like I apologize every time I look at you. I can't apologize anymore!" The words came out hot and clear. My ears buzzed even as the tips of them froze. Jules's eyes widened. The cloud in front of her mouth vanished. There was my old friend, alive and looking right at me.

"Hey, I didn't do anything," Jules said in a fierce whisper.

"Ignoring me is not *nothing*. Excluding me is not *nothing*. I'm done walking on eggs!"

"You mean eggshells?"

"I mean what I mean," I said, because even if I'd gotten the expression wrong, eggs, with all their gooey, messy insides, seemed much worse to walk on than shells. "I can't keep feeling like I owe you something."

"*I* can't help how *you* feel," she said.

"Well, I'm done acting like I've committed the crime of

the century." I picked up my stick and kicked off the dirt.

"Okay," she said.

"Okay?"

Miss Kang jogged over. "What's the verdict?"

"We're in," Jules said, wiping her mouth guard on her kilt.

"Are you sure?" she asked.

"Definitely," I added before the wind had a chance to shift.

"Get over there and talk to your team." Miss Kang gestured to the amorphous pack of girls standing dejectedly around the giant watercooler, sucking on orange slices, shivering, stealing cautious glances in our direction. "Seriously, give them a pep talk."

We didn't score in the second half, but neither did Peabody, and by the end of the game, their coach had subbed back in at least half of their starting lineup. Miss Kang called it a dignified loss.

From that moment on, we had a truce. We could lead our team, hang out in groups, or even be paired up for the Rosewood Cares Food Drive table at the street fair, but we had to obey three simple rules. One, we didn't talk about her mom. Two, we didn't talk about Nantucket, not about her wild, partying ways, not about her mean streak, as bright as a gasoline path aflame, or about her ditching me for Parker Carmichael, the mean-girl senator's daughter. And three, we never, ever talked about Zack.

Four

ONE SATURDAY IN NOVEMBER, I WAS STUDYING FOR MID-
terms at The Coffee Exchange. Brown and RISD students
had commandeered the place, and were huddled over text-
books, laptops, and sketchbooks. I saw Jules come in with
the leather backpack Nina had bought her in Italy. She
looked around for a spot, but every seat was taken. I waved,
pushed my stuff aside, and made room for her.

"I'm so glad you're here. I'm totally lost with European
History," she said and dropped her bag, with a thud. She
found the one empty chair in the whole place and carried it
over her head across the room to our table. "'Scuse me," she
said to a bearded drama student as she lowered the chair next
to me. He gave her a dirty look and tweaked his handlebar

mustache. "What?" she asked him; then she turned around, pulled out her European History folder, and sighed.

"Which prompt did you pick?" I asked.

"The one on world markets?"

"That's the hardest one. Let me see your notes."

After almost three hours of drinking too much coffee, consuming two giant pieces of cinnamon cake each, and mapping out our essays, we decided to reward ourselves with a movie at the Avon. Since they showed only one movie at a time, we had to see whatever was playing. It was a weird Danish murder mystery set in a 1970s nudist colony, told from several naked perspectives. We were dying of laughter at all the flapping boobs and bobbing penises, even though the ten other people in the movie theater were very serious.

After, we went to CVS, even though neither one of us had anything specific to buy, and tried to figure out who the killer was.

"It had to be the guy with the man boobs," she said as she sniffed a new brand of shampoo.

"No, it was the lady with all the . . ." I said, and gestured in front of my crotch.

"That's it! She hid the weapon in her bush!" We doubled over in laughter. She handed the shampoo to me to sniff. "Is it just me or does this smell like poop?"

"Ew!" I said, pushing it away, "I don't want to sniff it." We kept bumping into each other as we meandered toward the magazines. We discussed everything from the latest teacher gossip (Miss Kang was dating Señor Rodriguez again) to the best type of jeans for our butts, to the subtle British accent one of our classmates had picked up on a recent trip to London. We sampled body lotions until our hands were sticky. They smelled like lavender and medicine and roses and grandmas. We pushed up our sleeves and sampled more on our forearms. We decided the apricot one was the best and slathered it up to our elbows. By the time we left, it was dark and we reeked of synthetic sweetness.

"So, who do you have your eye on this year?" she asked as we lingered outside CVS with mascara, some hot pink lip gloss, *Teen Vogue*, *Lucky* magazine, Red Vines, Junior Mints, and Fresca, which we'd long ago deemed the world's most underrated soda.

"No one," I said, realizing that she thought Zack and I had broken up. I opened my mouth to speak, but changed my mind. I didn't want to correct her and explain that we had "paused," because having my old best friend back, even for a day, felt like returning home, setting down a heavy suitcase, and curling up in a favorite chair. "How about you?"

"Actually," she said, sticking her hands deep in the pockets of her puffy jacket. "I kind of like Jay."

"Really?" I'd had a crush on Jay Logan from the eighth grade until last summer. It was weird to think of Jules liking him, only because of the time I'd invested in studying him, memorizing his lacrosse statistics, and daydreaming about our life together as a private school power couple. I still claimed him out of habit.

"Do you care?" she asked. Did I feel a pinch? A pang?

A twinge? Nope. Zack had turned my Jay Logan crush into ancient history.

"Not at all. Go for it." Strands of soft rock blew out of the glass doors as a group of guys carrying Brown University ice hockey equipment bags exited, dropping f-bombs and potato chip crumbs.

"Cool," she said. After our summer, it surprised me that she would care how I felt about the whole thing, but her shoulders sank with relief. Her eyelids fluttered and she smiled one of her huge, movie star smiles. It felt so good to give her something she wanted. "Good. 'Cause I think he likes me, too."

"That's great," I said.

"I'm going to call him tonight," she said, rocking on her heels.

"Do it!"

I took the shortcut home through the Brown athletic complex. Warm gusts of chlorinated air wafted from the aquatics center as I tightened the straps on my backpack. I skipped across the playing fields. The motion detector lights illuminated my path in brief, consecutive bursts.

That night I was sitting at my desk memorizing French verbs when my phone vibrated, panicking on the hard surface of my desk. I saw Zack's name, grabbed the phone, and stared at the screen as the buzzing traveled from the phone up my arm, and to my heart. He was breaking our rule. But I had to pick up. It was Zack. *Zack.*

"Hello?"

"Hey, beautiful." His voice wrapped around me like a summer breeze.

"What are you doing?" I asked, absurdly alert.

"I'm calling you," he said.

"Oh." I slid off my chair and expanded like a starfish.

"I'm coming home for Thanksgiving, and I want to see you."

"Me, too," I said, curling up, closing my eyes, and imagining him next to me.

What would I do if I saw him? I would sneak him into my room and hide him under my quilt. No, I would run away with him to Newport and we would get a room at a motel. No, at an inn with a fireplace and one of those big bathtubs. We would take wintery walks on the beach and eat clam chowder, sitting on the same side of the booth at the Black Pearl. I touched my face at the thought. My hands still smelled like the lotion Jules and I had sampled. I sat up and saw the CVS bag with the mascara and the magazines and the Junior Mints. "But Zack, I don't think it's a good idea."

"Are you kidding? It's the best idea. And I need to see you," Zack said. "I want to get back together. I want to do the whole long distance thing with texts and phone calls and Skype and bus rides."

"Um, I don't know."

"Please," he said. "This isn't working for me."

"It's not working for me either, but . . ." I held my breath.

I couldn't finish the sentence. I wanted so badly to see him. I wanted to spend the next few days tingling in anticipation.

"But what?" Zack asked.

"But, Jules," I said, on the verge of tears. If Jules and I could get through high school, we would be okay; everything changes in college anyway. But if Zack and I got back together now, Jules and I would be right back where we started. I'd be alone again.

"And what if I can't handle saying good-bye to you again?" I asked, realizing that Jules was only half of it. It'd been so hard to say good-bye once. It hurt again already, and we were still on the phone. How could I go through that over and over again for the rest of the year, wondering all the time if he was thinking of me, too; waiting for him to call; analyzing his Facebook posts? No, I didn't want that. I just wanted to be with him in person, the whole summer in front of us like that dream where the house keeps going, each step revealing better rooms, bigger windows, balconies, pools, gardens. "Just wait for the summer. The summer is our time."

"So you don't want to see me?" he asked.

"We'll be back together in June," I said, hoping it would soothe the panic in his voice.

"I can't wait," Zack said. "I can't put my life on pause."

"It's only temporary." It was easy to think that long distance would work on a cold November night a week before he was coming home, but one of us had to stay strong. "I love you, Zack. My feelings aren't going to change. I know it."

"I love you, too," he said.

I felt a "but" dangling at the end of the sentence, like a loose tooth, but I told myself I was imagining it.

Five

I WOKE UP ON CHRISTMAS MORNING AND REALIZED I'D forgotten to buy my stepmother's parents a gift. Dad had given me a speech about how Polly's parents, Rosemary and Jim, had made a big effort to include me as their grand-daughter. They'd given me a set of monogrammed towels for no apparent reason the last time I visited them. We were going to their house for Christmas dinner and he was depending on me to be a *thoughtful, responsible* person, the kind of person who didn't buy Christmas presents at CVS on the actual day, as I had done last year for Polly and Alexi. This year, I'd remembered to get Polly a special kind of pan for angel food cake and Alexi a package of glow-in-the-dark stars for his ceiling (with a book about constellations) last weekend, but I had totally spaced on Rosemary and Jim.

I had an excuse. I'd just turned in my college applications. They were so refined and sparkling they were like compressed, digital jewels. I even had a letter of reference from George Gust, the journalist I'd interned for last summer on Nantucket, that was so awesome my mom wanted to frame it. I submitted all my applications two weeks early. But I still had to get a present for Polly's parents.

Starbucks was open on Christmas and it was a step up from CVS, and two whole blocks closer, which, considering it had snowed three feet the night before, was a big plus. No one had shoveled, so I was in it up to my knees, making deep, fresh footprints, and climbing snowbanks at the curbs. Everything was cold and glinting, but with all the heaviness at home, I wasn't feeling the magic.

Mom had exclaimed at least three times that "we girls" were a "perfect team" and "fine just the two of us." No pill and no amount of chardonnay was strong enough to dull Mom's pain at being single at Christmas, and yet she was pretending that I hadn't noticed how disappointed she'd been that, without Dad, there had been so little for her under the tree. Now I was dreading my performance in the second act of the Happy Divorced Christmas play. I couldn't wait for the day to be over. This wasn't how Christmas was supposed to feel.

It had actually started snowing again when I reached Starbucks, where a neat, straight path had been shoveled from the sidewalk to the entrance, and I reached out with a mittened hand to catch a fat, glimmering flake. Bing Crosby was being piped through the outdoor speakers. A little boy made a snowman in what was usually an ugly parking lot, but now looked like the top of a frosted cake. A couple passed by on cross-country skis. I smelled chimney smoke.

I was looking at the stuff on the back wall, trying to pick out the thing that would seem the least like I had bought it that morning. A French press? A set of travel mugs? Was there *anything* without the store logo on it? Did Rosemary and Jim even drink coffee? Then I spotted a monkey mug. The handle was the monkey's arm scratching his head. The monkey had a dopey expression, but it made me laugh. I was contemplating if they would like it too when the door swung open and I felt a rush of cold air. It was Zack. He wore a black wool peacoat and a red cashmere scarf. His cheeks were pink and there was fresh snow in his hair.

I stood frozen, aglow, a monkey mug in each hand. I must've been emitting some signal, because at that moment he turned to see me among the cappuccino machines, my mouth open like I was about to burst into "O Holy Night." When his eyes met mine, he blinked twice and smiled the warmest, biggest smile. I felt a drop of happiness enter my bloodstream so potent that a second one might have sent me to the emergency room for an overdose. I was wrong not to have seen him over Thanksgiving. I was so stupid not to do long distance. How could I have denied myself *this*? I wanted to feel *this* forever.

"Come here," he said. I ran to him, wrapped my arms around his neck. He hugged me so tight my feet lifted off the ground. His cold ear pressed against my hot face. I inhaled his scent—wet wool and pine—and he spread his hand over my back and held it there. It was Christmas in three heartbeats.

"Hey, you," he said.

"Hey, you, too," I said. My cheeks burned.

"What are you doing?"

"Christmas shopping," I said, shrugging.

"Pretty lame," he said with a smile, nodding at the mugs.

"I think they're cute." I imitated the ridiculous grin of the monkeys.

Then his phone rang. "I bet this is Jules, changing her mind again. Our plane leaves in two hours and the girl is acting like we have all day." His phone persisted, but he ignored it. "She's not even packed."

"Where are you going?"

The Claytons were not a travel-on-Christmas family. They were a stockings-filled-with-clementines-chocolates-and-new socks, homemade-actual-figgy-pudding, get-dressed-up-to-go-to-midnight-mass-but-just-for-the-music family. I loved how when I used to go over on Christmas my clothes would smell like the fire that had been burning in their house all day. The one we chucked our orange peels into.

"Mexico," he said. "Cancún. Dad surprised us at the last minute."

"Cancún?"

His phone rang again. He silenced it without looking.

"Time for a change," he said. His phone rang again. The

caller's third attempt. He checked it. His features subtly shifted. He turned away and picked it up.

"Hey," he said quietly, too quietly, into the phone. "You, too. Of course I miss you."

I didn't have to ask if it was a girl. I just knew in my bones. As I felt air vacuumed from my lungs, I made a promise to myself not to cry. Zack stepped out of line to take the phone call. I bought the mugs, handing the cashier a twenty-dollar bill with a shaking hand. She was asking me something about a receipt—did I want it e-mailed? I couldn't even hear her. I muttered, "No, thank you," and didn't wait for my change. I ran out of the store, leaping over the snowbank, immune to the chunks of ice in my socks and the wind chafing my cheeks.

It wasn't until Jim and Rosemary opened their presents at their house that I saw that the mugs were both emblazoned with the Starbucks logo on the back. I'd even left the prices on them, showing the Christmas discount. They told me how much they loved monkeys, how much they loved Starbucks. My dad shook his head. A minute later, while Alexi was stomping around with his new toy airplane, I excused myself and fled to what Rosemary called the powder room.

Zack had moved on. I'd let Dad down, again. Mom was alone. I was in a near stranger's house on Christmas.

"You okay in there?" Rosemary said, knocking gently at the door.

"I'm fine, thanks," I said, as politely as I could. I held a Christmas-themed hand towel to my face as I silently released the tears I'd been holding in since Starbucks.

January, February, and March dragged on like one of Edwina MacIntosh's lectures about cliques. That winter there had been one blizzard, two nor'easters, and three months of dirty slush. The bitter cold had somehow helped me perfect the art of not thinking about Zack. One bright spot had been when George Gust's book came out, the one he'd been writing last summer on Nantucket. He'd put my name in the acknowledgments just like he'd promised. He'd even given me my own sentence: *A big thank-you goes to Cricket Elizabeth Thompson, my faithful intern, for providing good sense, keen insight, and a steady supply of Coke Zero.* I couldn't believe my name was in a real book for the whole world to see. It got me through waiting to hear if I was going to Brown next year.

My acceptance to Brown was a golden ticket to the future. It arrived on a Saturday. Mom and I went out for dinner and she let me sip her champagne. On Sunday, Dad took me to Nordstrom and told me to pick out anything I wanted. I didn't tell anyone else I'd been admitted until the next Monday, when I marched right into the senior lounge and wrote *Brown* on that giant piece of butcher paper, smack in the middle. My classmates congratulated me, even as, in some cases, their eyelids beat double time with jealousy.

Ed invited me to her office for lunch. We ate with real silver forks and knives. Miss Kang did a victory dance in the middle of the cafeteria. Jules even picked me a bouquet of daffodils from the school's garden. But of course, the person I wanted to tell more than anyone was Zack.

Six

I SAT ON THE GRADUATION STAGE IN MY PAST-THE-KNEE white cotton dress, my hair swept up in a chignon, sweating under the hot June sun. I could hardly believe high school was over. The microphone squeaked as our commencement speaker, Richa Singh, class of 1991 and professor emeritus of astronomy at MIT, adjusted her sari, leaned in, and said, "Today I'm going to embrace the lesson Mrs. Hart taught me many years ago: above all, be succinct." It was eleven a.m. and nearly one hundred degrees.

The crowd, perspiring in a range that stretched from light dew to full-drenched soak, laughed. A hot breeze rustled the leaves of the huge copper beech tree behind the wooden platform where my graduating class sat in two neat rows. My mom caught my eye and waved from the audience. Brad, her boyfriend of four months, was next to her, wiping sweat from his brow with a handkerchief. Dad, Polly, and Alexi sat two rows back. Alexi's head was bent in rapt concentration as he played with his iPad. Dad pointed his fancy camera in my direction. I could see his huge smile under the long lens.

"When you see stars, you are looking into the past," Richa Singh began. "You see a celestial body, such as a star or a comet, as it was when the light coming from that body began its journey to your eye. It's possible when you look into the night sky you are seeing stars that no longer exist." It was too hot to wrap my mind around this, so I tuned out and scanned the crowd. I spotted Mr. Clayton sitting alone between two empty seats. It was as if he'd saved a seat for Nina, I thought, and I felt a bright wire of pain. It surprised me how it could still hurt this much, how pain that you think has dulled can come back so sharp, so fast, just to let you know it's still there. Where was Zack? How could he miss his sister's graduation? *How could he miss mine?*

"So, I know you've all heard about Larsen's Comet," Richa continued. "It's making its rounds for the first time since 1939. It will be particularly bright in the northeastern sky for the month of August, with a tail of a hundred degrees, which is big—trust me." She turned to address my classmates and me. "You literally have a bright future, a cosmic event as spectacular as you can hope to witness in your lifetimes. But here's the trick. You must be awake to the moment. You must get out from behind your screens and handheld devices, get away from city light pollution, and take in the sky. There's no picture, no text, no YouTube video that can compare to seeing it with your own eyes. The world offers us brilliance and beauty, but it is up to us to show up. So, go get 'em, grads! Reach for the stars!"

Everyone clapped, and Edwina MacIntosh approached the podium in her powder-blue suit. I took a deep breath, preparing for my big moment. "And now, as is tradition, the student council president will read a poem. This year's president is one of the girls I can proudly say has been at Rosewood since kindergarten. I'd like to think we take partial credit for what a remarkable young woman she has turned out to be. She's headed to Brown University in the fall, and last week, here on this very lawn, she was awarded the Sarah Congdon Award for student athlete demonstrating exceptional citizenship. Cricket Thompson, will you please come and read 'A Psalm of Life' by Henry Wadsworth Longfellow?"

I slid past my classmates, stood in front of the podium, and made eye contact with the crowd. *"Tell me not—"* I began.

That's when I saw Zack take the empty seat next to his dad. He was taller, bigger, further along the road from boy to man. What had been the beginning of a transformation at Christmas was now complete. He was no longer a dorky-but-hot-to-me sophomore. In his Nantucket Reds and a white button-down, with the sleeves rolled up, he was flat-out gorgeous. My mouth went dry. I had to start again.

"Tell me not, in mournful numbers, 'Life is but an empty dream!'
For the soul is dead that slumbers," I continued, clutching my
index card. *"And things are not what they seem."*

I think something happens after you've been in love with
someone, and especially if you've had sex, because I had a
GPS on Zack as my parents asked me to pose for various
pictures near the beech tree. Even when I was facing away,
smiling at the camera, I was aware of his presence. He was
over by the lemonade. He was texting. He was laughing at
something Jules said. Where were his glasses, I wondered?
Did he get contacts?

"Okay girls," Mom said, gesturing to Jules. "Let's get the
two of you."

Jules and I put our arms around each other, though not
as tight as we once would have. We tilted our heads toward
each other. I could feel that we were both holding our
breath as my mom and Mr. Clayton snapped pictures. Then
Mr. Clayton stepped forward and handed Jules a package
wrapped in white tissue paper and a single blue ribbon.

"This is for you," Jules said, handing the package to me.

"Oh," I said, taking the gift. "Thank you."

"It's from all of us," Mr. Clayton added, smiling, throwing an arm around Zack.

I unwrapped the tissue paper and gasped. It was a picture, in a simple, wooden frame, of Nina on her graduation
day from Brown. I'd seen the picture many times. It had
sat on Nina's dresser for as long as I could remember. Nina

was in her graduation gown. Her cap was off and her hair was long and flowing. She was looking right at the camera, daring me to do something great. I held the picture to my chest. "Thank you."

"Let me see," Mom said, taking it. "Aw," she cooed, as if it were a picture of a cute puppy. I snatched it back.

"Are you sure I can have this?" I asked. It was such a part of their home I felt like I was walking away with their chimney or the stained glass window in the dining room.

"She loved you, Cricket," Mr. Clayton said. For the first time I noticed how much he'd aged this year. "And she loved Brown. She would've been so happy you were going there."

I looked at Jules. A shade of hesitation passed over her face before she smiled and said, "Hey, it's not like I was going to get in."

"Thank you," I said, hugging Jules with all of my might. I took a step toward Zack, about to hug him, too, when he held up his hand.

"Hey, Cricket. Give me five."

Honestly, it would have been better if he'd told me to fuck off.

I held up a hand, not sure if I was going to give him five or slap him. Jules took my hand and spun me around, a residual friend instinct kicking in. "There's a party tonight at Jay's house," she said as she dipped me. "Pick you up at eight."

Seven

"WOULD YOU LIKE SOME DISGUSTING CAKE, MY LADY?" ALEXI asked, his cowlick pointed north and his lip curled in repulsion. Polly had given Alexi the job of waiter to keep him busy at my graduation barbecue.

"Alexi, that's not very nice," Polly said. "Kate made that cake for Cricket."

"Sorry, Kate," Alexi said, aware he'd socially misfired, something he was working very hard not to do.

"It's okay," Mom said, tousling his hair. She stage-whispered, "Carrot cake is Cricket's favorite, but I don't really like it either. Who wants vegetables in their cake?" She made a face, and Alexi laughed like this was the funniest thing he'd heard all year.

This was a huge improvement from how this evening had

started. I didn't think I was going to make it to eight p.m., when Jules had promised to pick me up. At one point, Dad asked Mom's permission to use the "restroom," even though it had been his *bathroom* in his house for fifteen years. He not only knew where it was, he knew what kind of soap would be by the sink and where the towel hanging on the rack had been bought.

And then, later, when Polly's parents gave me a set of some top-of-the-line monogrammed sheets as a graduation present, Mom whistled and said, "Wow. Those are nicer than the ones we got for our wedding, right, Jack?" Dad coughed, Rosemary pursed her lips, and I felt like I had to apologize. And then, after that, Brad tried to teach Polly the correct stance for fly-fishing when she clearly didn't want to learn, at least not in heels in my mom's backyard. She had to firmly tell him no for him to get the picture, and he'd flushed with such embarrassment he looked like a little boy.

But now it was seven fifty p.m., the barbecue was wrapping up, and everyone had consumed enough alcohol to at least be able to simulate a normal social gathering. Except for Alexi and me. Alexi was allowed only water to keep his sugar intake down, and I was sticking to lemonade for now, though I could've used something to help me forget about Zack's high five, which was hovering in the air over my head. It was like he'd forgotten who I was.

I wasn't the girl he high-fived. I was the one he whispered secrets to in the predawn hours, the one who could make him laugh with a single raised eyebrow. The one who understood what he had lost when he lost his mother. I was the girl he loved, or at least that's what I thought. When someone stops loving you, I wondered, does that mean they never really even started?

As this thought crept across my mind, Aunt Phyllis and Uncle Rob put their arms around me and started to tell me again what it was like to go to college in Northampton, Massachusetts, in the 1980s. Lots of plaid shirts, combat boots, and crazy parties that they were hinting involved group sex. Someone needed to cut them off before they got any more concrete with their details.

Just then Mom stepped up on the big, flat rock in her garden, tapped her wineglass with a plastic fork and announced, a bit tipsily, "I'd like to toast Cricket. I have no doubt she's going to take over the world. I am so, so proud of you, baby!"

Everyone lifted glasses in my direction. Dad whistled. Alexi whooped. I took a little bow.

"That said," she continued, "I'm glad she's staying at home. Not just in Providence, but right here in this house."

Brown had offered me a great financial package, but it didn't cover everything. My parents didn't have a lot of money, and I didn't want to graduate with student loans, so we'd decided I'd live with Mom. Living in the dorms and eating in the cafeteria would have cost almost twelve thousand dollars a year. That didn't include student fees or books for classes. At the end of four years, I'd have been lucky to be only fifty thousand dollars in debt, which Dad explained would keep growing over time. Both my parents were still paying off their student loans. It seemed stupid to go into debt when we lived so close to the Brown campus that I could walk to all my classes, watch the marching band pass our porch every Saturday morning, and hear the soccer referee's whistle from my bedroom window.

"I can't deny that I feel so good knowing my daughter is right downstairs if I need her, like I did today when she helped me pick out this outfit." She curtsied, and Brad whistled. "And if she needs me for girls' chats or love advice, I'll be waiting. Who knows, we might even end up going on some double dates. We'll be double trouble, right, honey?"

"That's right," I said, downing my lemonade to mask my panic.

"I have something to say here," Dad said. I'd only heard Dad make one toast. It was at his wedding to Polly, and he hadn't mentioned me. He took a sip of his beer, staring at it for a second before beginning. "A lot of folks send their kids to public school and save for college. That was our plan, but Cricket peed her pants every day of her first three months at William McKinley Elementary."

Alexi pointed at me and cackled, checking to see who else had caught this comic gem. Polly pulled him close to her and he giggled into her skirt.

"Well, it's true," Dad said. "We hated the idea that Cricket didn't like school. So we visited Rosewood, Kate's alma mater, even though we knew we couldn't afford it." Mom smiled, nodded, and drained her glass. "And Cricket cried when it was time to come home. She said, 'I can't go home, Daddy. School's not over yet.' So, Kate and I made a decision. That weekend we sold our brand-new minivan so that she could finish kindergarten at Rosewood."

I remembered the day we sold the van. I think I was so excited that we were going to start taking the bus that it never occurred to me we were broke.

Dad continued, "We kept saying just for elementary school, just to get her on the right track. But Cricket was doing so beautifully. 'Daddy,' she'd say when I picked her up from school, 'guess what I learned today?' As teachers, it made our hearts sing.

"So then we thought, let's take out an extra mortgage and get her through those horrible middle-school years. You know, cliques and first bras and all that." I instinctively crossed my arms in front of my chest. More cackles from Alexi. The rest were quiet, listening. "And when high school came around, well, I think we all saw today how much a part of that school she was." He turned to me. "We couldn't take you out, no matter the cost. I don't think they would've let us. You were practically running the place." He shrugged, grinning, acting out his helplessness in the face of my success. "We took out another loan."

"Sorry," I said. I don't know how I had thought two teachers were paying for my expensive private-school education, but I guess I hadn't wanted to think about it, and they'd never asked me to.

"I'm not saying this to make you feel bad. Let me finish. We just hoped, year after year, that it would all pay off.

We crossed our fingers with each tuition check that we were making the right decision. We bet on you, Cricket." Here he drew a shaky breath, held it, looked at me, and glowed. "And man, did we hit the jackpot. Honey, I couldn't be prouder of you. Brown University. Member of the lacrosse team. The Ivy League! This is my daughter," Dad said, wiping his eyes, raising his voice and pointing to me like I'd just won an Oscar. "My brilliant, beautiful daughter!"

"Thank you," I said as I handed my lemonade to Aunt Phyllis and threw my arms around Dad as everyone clapped. I buried my head in his chambray-covered shoulder and smelled his Old Spice. Alexi tried to come between us, but my dad told him this was a father-daughter moment.

"We didn't realize you weren't living in the dorms," Rosemary said a few minutes later. "That's why we got you the monogrammed sheets. So you wouldn't lose them in the school laundry. They're for an extra-long twin bed."

"I love them. And I think that's what I have, anyway." It wasn't true, but I knew monogrammed things couldn't be exchanged.

"But the dorms are such a big part of the college experience," Jim added. Dad had told me that Jim came from a very poor family in Boston, and that he had worked in a hardware store to put himself through law school at night. "It was an experience I made sure Polly had, since I didn't get to."

"And I'm grateful, Dad," Polly said, patting her dad's back. "Poor Dad. He paid so much, and I was, let's say, very social."

"And it wasn't exactly Brown," Jim said.

"I know Hamilton isn't Ivy League," Polly said, putting a hand on her hip. "But it's still a good school."

"I think we'd have to ask someone who actually attended class," Jim said.

"Ouch, Dad," Polly said.

"Polly, do me a favor and get me another piece of cake, hmm?" Rosemary said, then leaned in and whispered, "Gotta break these two up sometimes."

That's when Jules pulled up, but it took a minute to recognize her. She wasn't in the Audi or the land yacht. She was in a brand-new Jeep with a bright red ribbon on its hood.

Eight

"HEY, HEY," JAY SAID AS HE WALKED TOWARD US IN HIS rooftop living room and kissed Jules. "C.T." He pulled me close for a rough hug. "What's up, girl?" Jules made a bee-line for a well-known and deeply feared clique composed of three Alden girls: Chloe, Jessie, and Gemma. They greeted her with a collective shriek-giggle as she kicked off her sandals, poured herself a drink, and joined them on the sofa. As Jay's girlfriend, this was her party, too.

"What are you up to this summer, C.T.?" Jay asked.

"Working at Leo's," I said. Leo's was a sandwich shop between the Brown and RISD campuses, famous for its barrel of pickles. My first shift was in three days. For the first time, I didn't mind staying in Providence for the summer while all my classmates went off on some exotic adventure or to a second home in an elite location. I just wanted to start college.

"You're stuck in Providence?" Jay asked. "That sucks."

"I'm fine with it."

"Cool," Jay said. "I have an internship at my dad's bank in London."

"Wow," I said, as we made our way to the bar. "London." I felt a dagger of panic. Should I be going someplace like London this summer?

"And Jules, as you probably know, is—"

"Heading to Nantucket on Friday," Jules said, interrupting him.

I smiled and turned to greet the Alden Three. "Hey, Chloe; hey, Jessie; what's up, Gemma?" Gemma waved. Jessie nodded. Chloe mumbled hello.

"So here's the plan," Jay said, sitting next to Jules and squeezing her knee. "There's this secret old bowling alley in one of the old buildings at Brown."

"For real?" asked Gemma, whose heavy eyelids indicated she was already drunk.

"Yeah," Jay said. "It's from, like, the forties, and Dirt's brother knows how to break in." Rich Green, a.k.a. "Dirt," looked up through a haze of pot smoke and nodded. "So we're going bowling tonight, kids."

"It's fucking awesome," Dirt said. "They have pins and everything. And you have to go through these underground tunnels to get there." Then, noticing me for the first time, he smiled and meowed. I scooted a little farther down the couch, away from him.

"In your dreams, Dirt," Jay said. Dirt shrugged and spat.

"Dude," Jay said.

"That's brilliant," Jules said. "We have to make teams!"

"I don't know," I said.

"Don't worry," Jay said. "We're going to be quiet and cool, and no one's around. The campus is, like, dead."

A second wave of Alden kids arrived, busting through the door to the roof. "LO-GAN," Lucas Saunders shouted, pumping a fist in the air; his other arm was weighted down with a six-pack.

"I might have to sit this one out," I said.

"Oh, come on," Jules said. With the sunset behind her, she was outlined in gold. "You have to come."

"Think of it this way," Jay said, heading behind the bar and scooping ice into a plastic cup. "This is our last night of high school. Our whole life is about to change. What can I get you?"

"Just a Coke," I said.

He poured Coke into the cup, fastened a sliced lime to the rim, and handed it to me. "You only live once, right?"

"That's what they say, but I can't do it," I said.

Someone with squeaky brakes was parking on the street below. Jules tensed, stood, and peered over the edge of the rooftop, then turned around with a furrowed brow. "Ugh," she said, sinking back into her seat. "Ugh, I told them not to come."

I stood and saw the land yacht below. I held my breath as Zack stepped out of the car and judged his parking job. My heart hammered as my mind circled the pronoun *them*.

I watched as a girl climbed out of the passenger seat and combed her fingers through her dark, shiny hair. She was a little unsteady in her sky-high heels on the uneven sidewalk and Zack reached out a hand to her. As they joined hands and walked toward the front door, it sank in that Zack had a real, live girlfriend. She wasn't just a mysterious presence on the other end of a phone at Starbucks, but an actual person with fantastic hair. As I leaned farther over the railing to watch them walk, I realized I knew her. The air left my lungs as her familiar laugh drifted up from the street like a tendril of smoke.

His girlfriend was Parker Carmichael.

Nine

I FLEW BACK DOWN THE THREE FLIGHTS OF INCREASINGLY majestic stairs and out the oversize front door flanked by ceramic footmen. I just had to hope that Zack and Parker were taking the elevator. He wasn't going to have another chance to offer me a high five, not with Parker looking on. I knew they went to the same boarding school, but I never imagined they were together. I was in mid-driveway, almost clear of the bus-size Suburban, when I felt a hand on my shoulder. Jules.

"Cricket, don't go. It's our graduation night."

"What's up with Zack and your friends? First me, now Parker?" She laughed, but I wasn't joking. "Why is he with her?"

"She goes to Hanover, too," she said.

"She does? But Parker is so mean. She's the meanest girl I've ever met."

"I don't know about that." Jules held up her hands like the scales of justice. "It's not that she's mean. You don't really know her. You, like, can't be objective. She can be great when she wants to be, and she's been through a lot." Laughter spilled from the rooftop. "Come on, don't you want fun memories of tonight?"

"Why didn't you tell me about Parker?"

"I don't know. You guys were broken up."

"And what happened to his glasses?"

"He got LASIK."

For some reason, this felt like a betrayal. "I have to go. Thank you for the picture."

"I thought we could have a night like old times, but never mind. Do you want a ride?" She looked like she'd rather conjugate French verbs. In a prison cell. In Siberia.

"No thanks, I'll walk."

But as soon as I was out of sight, I ran. Instead of going home, I went to the track at Alden where my feet tried to keep pace with my heart. Had that been Parker on the phone at Christmas? That meant they'd been together for six months, at least. Six months was serious. I felt like I'd been punched. I kicked off my flats and ran on the grass. I hit my stride. What did they talk about? Did he go to her house in Connecticut on the weekends? Had they been back to Nantucket together? Had they had sex? Ugh. That was a stupid question. Of course they had. It wasn't just that he'd forgotten who I was, he'd forgotten who he was. Richa Singh had said that when you look at the stars, you're seeing what no longer exists. Was Zack like those stars, I wondered? Was he even there at all?

I'd completely sweated through my tank top when I decided to head home. I hadn't counted the laps, but I was sure I'd run at least four miles tonight. Maybe five. My flouncy skirt was clinging to my tingling quads, and though I couldn't see in the dark, I knew my feet were filthy with ground-in dirt and grass. *I have lots of parties ahead of me next year,* I told myself as I used the light on my cell phone to search the grass for my discarded shoes. *Parties full of people who don't give a shit about Nantucket.*

When I first stepped into Mom's house, I thought the TV was on. I heard kissing and moaning and wondered what channel Mom had been watching. Those *Lifetime* movies are getting pretty raunchy, I thought. It wasn't until I took a few extra steps toward the kitchen that I realized that these were live, real-time sex sounds coming from the living room sofa. It was almost like I was suffering a moment of complete disbelief so intense that it took me a regrettable extra minute to put it together. I held my breath and flung my hands over my ears.

"Cricket?" Mom asked.

I didn't answer. It would be better for her to think it was

a burglar. I tiptoed back out the door, wincing as it slammed shut behind me, and sat on the porch steps with my head between my knees.

"Cricket?" Mom asked, appearing in the doorway moments later, her bathrobe wrapped tightly around her. She sat next to me, radiating a warmth I didn't want to think about. I put my head in my hands. She ran a light hand over my back. "Honey, why are you sweating?"

"I went for a run," I said, and pulled away.

"At night?"

"Yes."

"That's odd."

"What can I say? It's been an odd night."

"Hmm. I think we should talk about this."

"No, we shouldn't," I said, shaking my head. "No need. I promise."

"Well, okay, if you say so," she said, but didn't move.

"I need to be alone right now."

She sighed and stood up, pausing in front of the door. "I almost forgot. You got a message."

"I did?" Zack, I thought in a flash of hope, calling to explain.

"It was Rosemary. She and Jim want to talk to you before they head back up to Boston tomorrow. She asked for you to meet them at Starbucks at nine."

"That's strange," I said.

"I'm going to go back inside now and Brad and I are

going to, um, retire to my bedroom. So you can feel perfectly comfortable coming back inside and—"

"Got it," I said. "I'm going to hang out here for a minute."

"You know, as roommates, we're going to have to learn
to, well, communicate about these things."

"Good night, Mom," I said. I shut my eyes and held my
breath until I heard the door shut behind her.

Ten

I'D ALREADY DOWNED HALF MY LATTE WHEN ROSEMARY
and Jim spotted me, waved, and joined me at the one free
table, which was really much too small for the three of us.
I hadn't slept well. I'd been so afraid of overhearing more
from Mom and Brad that it was like my ears were rebelling
and I'd become extra sensitive. I'd spent the night listening
to the walls breathe.

"We've been talking," Rosemary said.

"We're looking for a number," Jim said, rapping the table
with his knuckles.

"A number?"

"Honey, how much do you need to live in the dorms, eat
in the cafeteria, buy your books, and have some spending
money?" Rosemary asked.

"Oh. Well, I'm not sure." I gripped my latte. Were they offering what I thought they were? Did they have any idea how much money it would be? My parents and I had been over it a hundred times, and it was a lot more than any of us would've imagined. "It's a lot."

"This is no time to be shy," Jim said. He took a heavy gold pen from his shirt pocket and offered it to me along with a Starbucks napkin.

"Okay." I smoothed out the napkin. "The dorms are eight thousand." I drew an eight. "The meal plan is four." I added a four. "And anticipated student fees are two." I totaled it, writing *fourteen thousand* and turned the number to face them. "It's so much, it's really insane. I don't know how—"

"Let's add some spending money," Rosemary said. She crossed out my *fourteen thousand* and wrote *sixteen thousand*. She smiled. "A girl can't live on bread and lacrosse alone."

Jim peered down his nose through his glasses and studied the number. He rapped the table again. "Your father is a wonderful man. And he's done a world of good for Polly and the boy."

"Yes," I said.

"Now, I'm a businessman, a self-made businessman."

"His mother worked in the Necco Wafer factory," Rosemary said, patting his arm. "And his father drank her wages."

Jim raised a hand to stop her. "That doesn't mean I didn't get some help along the way. I did. And now I'd like to offer you some help and teach you a little about self-reliance."

"Okay." I was as ready to hear a plan as I'd ever been.

"If you make eight thousand dollars this summer, I'll match it," Jim said.

"Wow," I said. "That's so generous. Thank you."

"What do you think?" Rosemary asked. "Can you do it?"

"Of course," I said. "Absolutely."

"It has to be at least eight," Jim said.

"Got it," I said. "Eight."

"Then we've got a deal," Jim said. He stood up and shook my hand.

"You can use those sheets after all," Rosemary said as she kissed my cheek.

I watched in a stupor as they climbed into their Volvo and drove off, as if they went around changing lives on a daily basis. The amazement shifted to panic as I walked home. How was I going to do this? Eight thousand dollars in two months? Okay, two and almost a half, but still, it wasn't going to happen at Leo's for nine bucks an hour. Providence was hardly a summer destination. The restaurants were dead when the students were away. I mean, unless I aced an audition for the Legs & Eggs shift at the Foxy Lady. For a second I thought I could do it in secret and write a blog about it, but a second later I knew that was ridiculous. So, where was I going to get all that money?

When I got back home and saw Nina's picture propped up on my dresser, the answer came to me in a vision, the same way I imagine it does for religious people when they say they see the face of the Virgin Mary in a vegetable or a taco or whatever. Only it wasn't a holy figure that appeared before me, but a crescent-shaped island thirty miles out to sea. A place where money rolled in as thick as fog, where bills slipped through fingers like sand, where people's pockets were as deep and open as the ocean itself.

Nantucket.

Shit.

Eleven

THOUGH STARTING TOTALLY FRESH IN A NEW PLACE
might've been a good thing if I had had more time, with
just a little over nine weeks I needed to go where I knew the
lay of the land and had a few local references. This seemed
especially true once Liz, my British friend, with whom I'd
been a chambermaid at the Cranberry Inn last year, offered
to let me stay with her for a little bit. She was running the
place now because our old boss, Gavin, was off in Bali doing
yoga. She said I could crash in the manager's apartment with
her, but only for a week. After that, her boyfriend Shane was
moving in. "Waitressing is where the money is," she'd told
me. "Mark my words."

Over the next few days, I applied for ten waitressing

jobs through *The Inquirer and Mirror* Web site, picking the ones that came with housing. I'd even had a phone interview at a restaurant called Breezes, but I had failed the wine test. It was the first thing I had ever failed in my entire life. My lowest grade to date had been a seventy-eight. Clearly, if I was going to get a waitressing job, I needed to expand my wine knowledge beyond Mom's chardonnay with the kangaroo on the label, so I bought a book called *Wine Made Simple* and studied it every day with the same dedication I had once applied to SAT vocabulary words.

At the end of the week, Mom drove me to the Steamship Authority in Hyannis where I'd catch the ferry to Nantucket.

"You got everything?" Mom asked. People were sporting their brightest clothes and monogrammed canvas bags as they filed aboard *The Eagle* with their luggage, bikes, kids, and dogs. A man directed a line of Range Rovers, Jeeps, and Volvos onto the boat. It was chilly, windy, and spitting rain.

"I guess," I said, my mouth dry with anxiety.

"Here you go," Mom said and lifted my carry-on roller bag from the trunk. It was stuffed to the gills, mostly with shorts and T-shirts, but also with my running shoes and a comfortable pair of sneakers called Easy Spirits. They were the ugliest shoes I'd ever seen, but Mom insisted that there was no way to be a good waitress without comfortable shoes. She should know. She'd waitressed all through college and teacher school. I extended the handle and tilted it on its wheels. I slid my purse over my shoulder and tucked it safely under my arm. My picture of Nina was in there, and I didn't want anything to happen to it.

"Don't forget this," Mom said, handing me the lacrosse stick I'd almost left in the backseat.

"Oh, yeah, thanks. I'm going to need that." I had to practice my stick work. Stacy, the Brown lacrosse coach, was going to be posting weekly videos with practice drills, and we were supposed to be running an average of five miles a day. I stuck my lacrosse stick through a loop in my backpack.

"Well, I have one more thing for you," Mom said. "I figured since you found mine so interesting last year, you might as well write your own."

She handed me a package. I unwrapped it. It was a journal. It was dark purple with gold along the edges of the paper. It smelled like real leather. It felt solid, substantial. I put it in my purse with the picture. "Thanks, Mom."

"Oh, and I almost forgot. Paul said to call him if you need anything. He's out there pretty much full-time through August." She handed me the business card of Paul Morgan, the lawyer I met last summer on the island and tried to fix her up with before I realized he was gay. They were now Facebook buddies who always liked each other's posts. "Stick it in your wallet so you won't lose it. You're doing the right thing," Mom said, taking my face in her hands, "but it doesn't mean I can't be a little sad for myself. I was looking forward to us being roommates."

h, Mom. You and Brad are good together. You don't
e around."

at if I do? What if I need you?"

re going to be fine." I hugged her, grabbed my own
nd her back, and squeezed her tight.

ou're going to be fine, too. Aren't you and Jules
?"

' I said. I hadn't even told Jules I was going back
I kept making myself promise I was going to
nd of the hour, the end of the morning, the
ut here I was, about to get on the ferry, and
w.

ut Zack?"

bout that." I felt a wave of seasickness
," THE
ill on land.
he slid
's nothing more attractive than self-
ely. The

ng not to think of him at all."
bbed my
se." She fished around in her purse
icked the
As a teacher, Mom had a Sharpie
cket over,
her at all times. I was about to
oard. As I
t Parker when she uncapped the
d the deck,
number eight on my palm.
backpack.
eyes on the prize. Eight thou-
ned against
er watch as I studied the inky
ght. I slid to
-like move to date. "Honey,
calated from
ing to leave any minute and
my raincoat,

Twelve

"CALM DOWN MISSY, YOU'LL MAKE THE TWO O'CLOC[K]
Santa Claus look-alike at the ticket counter said a[s]
me my change and added, "but you'll have to step li[ve]
heavens are about to open."

"Thanks." I stuffed the bills in my pocket, gr[a]
roller bag, and pivoted toward the door. The rain s[]
pavement as I darted to the boat, handed my t[]
and clambered up the metal ramp, the last one a[]
yanked my bag over the gap between the ramp an[]
my lacrosse stick slipped out of the loop on my [].

I bent down to pick it up and my purse slam[]
the cold, wet deck. My picture of Nina, I thou[]
my shins. My hood fell off just as the rain es[]
shower to downpour. I shoved the purse inside[]

gathered my stuff as best I could, and pushed my way through the heavy door to the inside part of the ferry, where the air-conditioning, set to arctic frost, sent a chill down my back like a zipper.

The knees of my jeans were soaked through to the skin. Water dripped from my ponytail and the hem of my raincoat. I looked around for a seat, or at least a corner to shove my bags in while I tried to rescue the picture. As the steam whistle blew and we pulled away from the dock, the people who had missed the heavy rain settled in. Dry and comfortable, they removed their moisture-wicking jackets and opened hardcover books and well-respected newspapers. Kids stared into their iPads or lined up to order hot dogs while their parents typed into their phones. Chocolate Labs and golden retrievers curled on cozy fleece beds. I stood dripping in my own private puddle.

"Is someone sitting here?" I asked a guy whose guitar was taking up a seat.

He looked up, blinking, like I'd just startled him out of a dream. He was older than me, but not by much. He had messy dark blond hair with a few strands of gold and lines that went from the corners of his bright blue eyes to his cheeks. He was cute and he knew it. He smiled up at me, pulled out his earbuds, and asked, "What's that?"

"Is this seat taken? I mean, by anyone besides your guitar?"

"Oh, no," he said, laughing a little as he stood up to get his guitar. He was wearing a gray wool sweater with a hole in the elbow. There was paint on his jeans and a little in his hair. As he leaned over to place his guitar under the seat, his T-shirt lifted, exposing a tan, muscular back. Was he doing that on purpose? "Looks like you're headed to the island for a while."

"Yeah," I said, arranging my stuff in an awkward pile.

"Me, too," he said. "What are you going to be doing?"

"Working," I said, peeling my dripping jacket off. "You?"

"Working, yeah, but also just taking it all in. Surfing. Writing music. Resetting, you know? There's nothing like a summer on Nantucket to shake things up."

"That's true," I said, thinking about how last summer had completely changed my life. "Um, can you watch my stuff?"

He patted my suitcase. "I'll guard it with my life."

A little girl sucking on a Popsicle watched with interest as I held the picture over the trash can and freed it from its ruined case. I brushed it off with the soft, dry sleeve of my sweatshirt. The photo looked so small and vulnerable without the frame, but except for a tiny corner piece that had torn off with an apple-seed of glass, it had survived. I turned it over to check the back and gasped. Written in faint ballpoint pen was a list.

Nina's Life List
1. *Visit Rodin Museum in Paris.*
2. *Learn to drive and then drive Route 1 to Big Sur.*
3. *Drink Campari on Amalfi Coast with Alison.*
4. *Be in a Woody Allen movie.*
5. *See St. Francis from altar.*

I traced my finger over her familiar architect's handwriting. I felt Nina's presence for the first time since her death. It was like she was leaning on the counter wearing brown duck boots and a Fair Isle sweater, her hair down and her brown eyes laughing at my discovery.

I'd never heard of this list before, and I wondered where and when she'd made it. Since it was on the back of her graduation picture, it must've been right after she'd finished Brown. They all had a check mark next to them except that last one: *See St. Francis from altar.* Maybe it was the faintness of the ink, or the small, girlish hearts drawn in each corner, or the checks next to the first four items on the list, each marked by a different pen, but I had a feeling that no one else knew about it. It was her secret, and now it was mine.

I stepped outside. The air was balmy compared to the dank, clammy cabin, and the rain was now a hesitant drizzle. I stood under the overhang and studied the list again, considering the first item. *Visit Rodin Museum in Paris.* Nina had spent a year in Paris after college graduation. I Googled it on my phone. The museum itself seemed grand but human-size, with ivy-covered walls, wooden-floored galleries, and huge, arched windows that opened. There were gardens divided by neat, leafy pathways and a reflecting pool. I scrolled through the collection. There was one sculpture called *The Walking Man.* It was a headless body of a man, well, walking. The body was so exquisitely defined, so muscular, so alive. *The Walking Man* is a hottie, I thought.

Then I saw the sculpture called *The Kiss.* My breath

caught. The way the man was holding the woman's hip, how they leaned back, the tilt of her head. It reminded me of Zack. It reminded me of what it was like to want someone so badly you feel every cell in your body turn to face him like a field of sunflowers. That's what we felt, I thought. No matter whom he was going out with now or the high-five crime, he had touched me like that. He had leaned like that. I knew it and he knew it. *Don't do it, don't do it,* I told myself. *Don't think about Zack.* I shut my eyes and started counting backward from one hundred by twos until the feeling passed, a trick I'd learned sometime after Christmas.

Thirteen

"THERE YOU ARE," A VOICE SAID. "BETTER GRAB YOUR STUFF, we're almost here."

"Huh?" I said, opening my eyes to bright sunshine. Guitar Guy was standing over me. How long had I been asleep? Two hours? Twenty minutes? I looked around to get my bearings. The deck was crowded, and we were almost at Brant Point. The lighthouse greeted us in its snappy white jacket and black top hat.

"We're almost to Nantucket. And you got a sunburn."

"Where?" I asked, blinking awake. My lips were dry. I needed some water.

"There," he said and gently touched the tip of my nose.

"Oh," I said, covering my nose with my hand. "Oh."

He didn't seem to think anything of it. He tipped his

face to the sun and said, "Don't you love how the weather on Nantucket is almost always the opposite of the mainland?" When I didn't respond he turned to me, grinned, and bit his lip as if trying not to laugh.

"What?"

"You're adorable."

"Thanks for waking me up," I said, standing and straightening my sweatshirt, which had twisted during my nap. "But you really shouldn't go around touching people's faces."

"I'm sorry. It's just that you—" He was trying not to laugh.

"It's actually really rude."

"You're right," he said, giggling.

"I'm going to Brown University in the fall." I'm not sure why I said this except I wanted him to know that I was a serious person, an *Ivy League woman*. But now he was laughing harder.

"Excuse me," I said and went back inside to get my stuff.

The ferry pulled in to the harbor and I strapped on my backpack, secured my lacrosse stick, and dragged my bag out from the spot I'd wedged it into. As I stood in the line of people impatient to get off the boat, I used the camera on my phone to check my sunburn. That's when I saw that my nose wasn't just red. Oh, no. Its tip was bright blue. *Of course.* The eight my mom had drawn was smudged and running and I had rubbed it off on my face. As I tried to wipe off the perfect circle of blue on the tip of my nose, my face burned red around it. Had I really needed to brag about Brown?

"Cricket!" I heard Liz call, and I searched the crowd for her. The dock was now a beehive of sherbet-colored pants as people reunited with friends, relatives, and luggage. I was almost the last one off the boat. Even though I'd wiped every trace of blue off my nose with the help of a brown paper towel and some pink industrial soap in the bathroom, I didn't want to run into Guitar Guy again.

"Cricket, over here!" Liz's voice seemed to rise above the others and lift me an inch off the ramp, but I still didn't see her. What a difference this was from last year when no one was there to meet me.

"Liz!" I called when I finally spotted her, arms waving overhead like a drowning woman. I darted through the crowd and hugged her. She smelled exactly the same, like rose perfume and cookies, but she was dressed like a different girl. Gone were the jean shorts and neon-colored bra straps. Liz had gone business casual in a navy knee-length skirt and a white button-down blouse. At least her jewelry was still Liz-style. Big red earrings and matching plastic bracelets.

"You look so proper," I said.

"Well, I'm the manager now, aren't I? I need to look responsible. And what about you? Turn 'round."

"What? Why?"

She motioned for me to hand her some luggage. I gave her my backpack.

"Panty-line check. Go on. I want to know how my pupil has fared without my guidance." I sighed and did a little turn for her. "Well done." She put on my backpack, handling my lacrosse stick like it was a strange artifact. "And is this a weapon? Gavin left his rain stick in the cupboard. We can have a battle!"

"It's my lacrosse stick," I said, taking it back. "I need to practice, like, a lot."

"I'm kidding. You don't think I could live on Nantucket and not know what lacrosse is, do you?"

"I never know what you know or don't know." Liz could explain the rules of American baseball with absolute clarity and knew certain Nantucket billionaires on a first-name basis and three good ways to create a smoky eye, but she didn't know how to ride a bike or why, exactly, we celebrated Thanksgiving.

"Someone's got to keep you on your toes. Come on now," she said, linking her arm through mine. "We've got to get back to the inn. I have a couple coming in on a flight from New York, and I need to be there when they arrive. The Nutsaks."

"That's not their name," I said, laughing.

"N-U-T-S-A-K, from the eastern bloc, perhaps? And I've got to have the balls to look them in the eye and welcome them." We laughed as we wove through the SUVs driving off the boat and walked into town. The scent of waffle cones wafted from the Juice Bar. I drifted toward it, but Liz pulled me back.

"But there's hardly a line," I said. "And there's *always* a line."

"I have to get you stowed away before the guests arrive."

"But chocolate peanut butter cup in a waffle cone . . ."

"Soon enough," she said, steering me onward. "I haven't even heard about your love life yet."

"Nothing to tell," I said. "Zack is going out with Parker Carmichael."

"Bastard!"

"I don't want to talk about it."

"Very well."

I was grateful for her British reserve as we headed up Broad Street and the old sights came into focus. It was busy, though not nearly as busy as it was going to be in July and August. I saw the bench where I'd eaten pizza alone my first week here. I hadn't known what else to do for dinner. There was the corner where Jules had pretended not to see me, her hair flying from the passenger side of a Jeep blaring a hip-hop song I hadn't recognized.

My heart sped up when I saw the tiny, hidden-in-plain-sight park where Zack had first held my hand in public. The very late-afternoon June light was as yellow as lemon cake, and green leaves and small blooms were climbing the gazebo, creating a woody, magical frame for kissing. The memories were flying in like slanted raindrops through an open window, and I was powerless to stop them. How was I going to make it through this summer knowing Zack was here in our paradise but no longer mine? How was I going to make it to the inn? We hadn't even hit Main Street yet.

Just as we were rounding the corner of Centre Street, I caught a glimpse of Guitar Guy stepping out of a bakery with a coffee. He seemed to be smiling at nothing in particular as he removed the lid of his coffee cup to blow into it. He sat on a shady bench and tapped something into his phone.

"Turn back," I said under my breath.

Liz followed me back down Broad Street. "What's gotten into you?"

"I met that guy on the ferry," I whispered.

"The bloke with the coffee? He's quite fit."

I shushed her, but that only made her louder.

"Okay, what's the story? Did you leave your knickers on the ferry? Is that why you have no panty line? Please say yes. Then the pupil will have surpassed the master, like in the movies."

"No, no. It was nothing."

"Doesn't seem like nothing," she said, and pinched my butt. Where was her British reserve now?

"What about you, sex goddess?" I asked, changing the subject. "How's your love life?" Liz and her Irish boyfriend, Shane, had practically been living together when I left Nantucket last summer. During our mornings of scrubbing bathrooms and making beds, I'd endured endless stories of their cinematic sex, his intense understanding of great poetry, and his taste for complex whiskey. They were so into each other they'd decided to stay on Nantucket together through the winter instead of returning to the UK, so I was surprised when the briefest shadow crossed her face before she answered, "Ace."

Fourteen

"GET UP!" LIZ SAID THE NEXT DAY. SHE HANDED ME A CUP of coffee with cream and no sugar, remembering just how I liked it, and a cranberry walnut muffin. It took me a minute to register that I was on the sofa in the manager's apartment. It was still weird to me that this was where Liz lived now. Last year, this was the boss's apartment and we lived in tiny single rooms with a shared bathroom. "For a girl who needs a job you've certainly had a lazy morning," Liz said. I sipped the coffee and glanced at the clock. It was almost ten thirty.

"Oh, shit!"

"Oh, shit, is right," she said. "You have a job interview this morning at one of the island's most expensive and popular restaurants. So eat up. We can't have your energy flagging."

"What?" I almost choked on a walnut. "Where?"

"Three Ships."

"Liz!" I gasped, spilling a bit of the coffee down my new Brown Women's Lacrosse T-shirt. Three Ships was on the wharf and had amazing views of the waterfront. It was almost impossible to get a reservation.

"Waitresses make three hundred dollars a night," she said and I gasped again, "And the position comes with housing."

"You're the best. Thank you! How did you do this?" I asked as I stuffed the muffin in my mouth. A job at Three Ships was the best-case scenario.

"I just ran into Charlie, the manager, at the pharmacy. I told him to look out for an athletic blond named for an insect. He said to come by at eleven a.m."

I glanced at the clock above the TV. "Jesus. That's in, like, twenty minutes. I've got to get changed. I haven't even showered yet."

"No time for a shower. A whore's bath, maybe."

"A horse bath?"

"*Whore's* bath. The bath of a whore. You know, prostitute? Sex for money?"

"Yes, I'm familiar with the term *whore*, but . . ." I threw the covers off, hopped into the bathroom, and turned on the water. "Never mind."

"One little thing," Liz said as I stepped into the shower. "I kind of told him you worked in New York for a year."

"What?" I grabbed the shampoo.

"Oh, now, don't say it like that. He said he wanted someone with experience. What was I supposed to do?"

"Where did you tell him I worked?"

"The Russian Tea Room," Liz said. "I was really thinking on my feet."

"What's that?" I pictured furry hats and elaborate porcelain teapots as I rinsed my hair. No time for conditioner. I quickly washed my pits and shut off the water. "Can I have a towel?"

"It's legendary, a really excellent place to have worked," she said, opening the curtain and handing me a towel. "Nice tits, by the way."

"Um, thanks." I grabbed the towel and covered myself. "But, Liz? I've never even been to the Russian Tea Room. I've only been to New York once. For the day."

"Improvise! Do you want to get the job or not?" She glanced at her watch. "Oh, you'd better hurry. And a little mascara never hurts, yeah?"

I made it to Three Ships by ten fifty-nine, in my neatest-looking shirt and skirt, combed, damp hair, and a little mascara.

"You must be Cricket," said a handsome man who looked like he'd just stepped off of a sailboat.

"And you must be Charlie," I said. We shook hands and he led me to a table by a window.

"So, tell me all about the Russian Tea Room," he said.

"It's an extraordinary place," I said, doing my best not to lie. I'd Googled it on the way there and memorized a few details. "It's so centrally located. So opulent. So famous."

He smiled, tapped his pencil on the table. "What was your favorite dish?"

"The chicken Kiev," I said, maintaining cheerful eye contact.

"The Kiev, huh? How would you describe it?"

"I would describe it as delicious." I closed my eyes as if imagining the experience. "Just so, so delicious."

"How many tables were in your section?"

"Twenty?"

"You must be some waitress." He smiled, leaned forward, drummed the table. "Did you really work at the Russian Tea Room? The *opulent, famous, centrally located* Russian Tea Room?"

"I've never even been there," I said. He laughed, so I did, too.

"Do you have *any* restaurant experience?" he asked.

"No," I said. "But I'm going to Brown in the fall. So I'm a really quick study."

"Impressive."

"And I'm on the lacrosse team, so I'm quick on my feet, too."

"But that also means you'd take off before Labor Day." I shrugged. "I can't hire you. For what people spend here, I need a professional staff. We get slammed. Tonight we have almost two hundred covers and . . ."—he paused, tilted his head—"You don't even know what that means, do you? Yeah. I'm not looking for someone to train from scratch."

"Do you know anyone who might be?" I asked. "Because the thing is, I really need a job this summer."

"Have you thought about retail? A lot of girls like you do that in the summer."

"Girls like me?"

"You know, Ivy League, blond, Daddy's got a place in town."

"You've got me all wrong. Girls like me need to make real money," I said and sat up a little straighter. "I may not have a lot of waitressing experience, but I worked at the Cranberry Inn last summer six days a week. I served breakfast every morning at seven a.m. sharp and cleaned rooms all day after that. I wasn't late once, and when a guest asked me for something, I always did my best to make sure I got them what they needed. I even ended up with an internship with one of them, a famous writer. And I'm not afraid to clean a bathroom. I'd rather not. But I will." I wrote my name and number on a napkin and handed it to him. "If you hear of anything, please pass on my number."

I walked toward the door, but Charlie's voice stopped me. "Well, I feel like a first-rate asshole. You look the part, but I shouldn't have assumed." He grabbed two bottles of fancy carbonated lemonade from behind the bar, uncapped them with some unseen device, and handed one to me. "I still can't hire a waitress without fine-dining experience, but my buddy Karla is still looking for someone and she's a little more open-minded." He wrote *Breezes, Jefferson Road* on a cocktail napkin. "Tell her I sent you."

"Thanks." I was going to mention that I'd already had a phone interview with Karla and she'd rejected me, but I changed my mind. Sometimes you have to take a few shots on goal before you score.

Breezes was about a mile outside of town, right on the sand. From the outside it looked like a beach house. I could smell the ocean from the wooden-planked pathway. The restaurant name was etched in gold above a bright blue door. It was the restaurant attached to the island's most exclusive beach club, the Wampanoag Club, or the Wamp, as everyone who knew better called it. People were on the waitlist for twenty-five years or more to get in, and I could see why. With its graceful shingles, welcoming porch, combed beach, and cozy cabanas, it was the perfect picture of a classic New England summer. Even from the outside there was a casual elegance that filled you with a sense that this could be your home in some alternate universe where you were so rich you could fling fistfuls of money at the sunset as part of your evening prayers.

The inside was pure Nantucket. The opposite of the Russian Tea Room, there was nothing opulent about this place, unless you counted the ruby-pink beach roses on every table, or the sapphire-bright hydrangea blooms on the hostess stand. The wooden floors were white. Brightly painted oars hung on the pale blue-gray walls. In the middle of the room was a smooth, gleaming bar, and beyond that a giant wraparound porch, protected from the elements by sheets of canvas-trimmed plastic, secured to the frame like sails to a mast. There was a jar on the hostess's stand labeled OPERATION SMILE. PLEASE DONATE. I picked up a menu. The least expensive thing was a twenty-three-dollar artisanal grilled cheese.

"Hello?" I asked, and when no one answered, I stepped out on the porch, which faced the Nantucket sound in three directions. It couldn't be denied that it was a beautiful place, even on a foggy day like today. With the exception of perfectly spaced-out yellow and blue beach umbrellas, all slanted at the same angle, the view was identical to the one at Steps Beach, where Zack and I had spent so much time together last summer. *Don't think of Zack,* I told myself. *Don't. He doesn't deserve it.*

"A million-dollar view, right?" I turned to see a small, sinewy woman my mom's age with bright blue hair framing eyes so brown they were black. Bright blue hair is not something you see every day on Nantucket. "What can I do for you? We aren't open until noon."

"Actually, I'm looking for a job. My name is Cricket Thompson." I winced. I was hoping she wouldn't be able to place me, but people don't forget a name like mine.

"I already interviewed you, didn't I? Yeah, I remember. You bombed the wine test. Like"—she made explosion sounds with the accompanying hand gestures—"bombed."

"Charlie from Three Ships sent me," I said. "He thought I'd be a good fit."

"Is that so?" She pushed her glasses up on her head like a headband. "You didn't tell me you knew Charlie."

"And I've been studying. Ask me anything." *Please, make it easy.*

"Okay. What would you recommend with a lobster roll?"

"Pinot grigio, to cut through the richness." I was ready for that one. On Nantucket, lobster rolls were as ubiquitous as sand.

"Good." She drummed her fingers on the bar. "How about the roasted-pig confit?"

"A French pinot." According to *Wine Made Simple*, French pinot was almost always a good choice.

"Well done. You have been studying. One more." *Don't let me down, Wine Made Simple.* "Hamachi crudo, our most popular dish this summer."

What the hell was hamachi crudo? I swallowed, and remembered that the book said that when in doubt, the best wine to order was simply one you enjoyed, no matter the dish. The best drink I'd ever had was champagne, last summer, on the Fourth of July, in a little rowboat with Zack.

"Dom Perignon," I said.

Karla's face opened up in a smile. "Best answer yet."

"I know I can do this. I really think you should give me a chance. I'm an athlete, so I'm used to working under pressure."

"An athlete, huh?"

"I'm playing lacrosse at Brown in the fall."

"All right, Cricket Thompson, I'll give you a shot."

"Yay!" I actually jumped.

"Calm down. We'll give it a week. See how it goes."

"Thank you so much!"

"Staff dinner is at four. See you then."

"Tonight?"

"Is that a problem?"

"Not at all," I said, though I still needed to go for a run and practice stick drills. She ducked behind the bar and tossed me a T-shirt the same shade as the famous Nantucket Red pants. "The first shirt is on the house. After that they're twenty bucks. You got a pair of khakis?"

"I can find some," I said.

"Four o'clock," she said. Her phone rang.

"Oh, and um, I need housing, too. That's what the original ad said?"

"I'll see what I can do." She saw the number on the caller ID, muttered something under her breath, picked it up, and spoke into the phone in rapid-fire Spanish. She handed me employment forms and gestured at the door.

It's just nine weeks, I told myself as I pulled on the last of several pairs of khakis in the Nantucket Hospital Thrift Store dressing room. *And then I'll be at Brown.* I sighed at my reflection in the mirror. Nothing could make these pants look good. The waist was high, and not in a cool retro way, and they were a little too short. But they basically fit otherwise and would have to do until Mom could send me a better pair from home. I'd tried Murray's first, the store famous for Nantucket Reds. I'd found a pair that were actually almost flattering, but they were a hundred dollars.

I wandered over to the thrift store, where secondhand khakis seemed to grow like weeds. I found at least six pairs in my size, four of which didn't have stains, and two of which were from this century. "Those are half off," the elderly thrift store volunteer said when I set them on the card table with the cash box and old-fashioned adding machine, the same one I'd seen Rosemary use to balance her checkbook. "All ladies' trousers are."

"I guess I'll get them both," I said.

"You sure you don't want to check out the books? Hardcovers are a dollar today. I can put these aside for you," she said, checking the labels as she folded the pants. "Oh, Talbots. You're lucky. The good brands go quick. I'll put these out of sight so no one snags them."

"Thanks." I smiled, not having the heart to tell her that the Talbots pants would probably have been safe even if they had been displayed on their one mannequin. I ducked into the book room and spotted a display of oversize art books. Even though they varied in size and style, I could tell they'd inhabited the same space for a long period of time. I imagined they had all been donated from one person's collection, some very dedicated museum lover. One was from the Getty in Los Angeles, one from the Frick in New York, and another was from the Rodin Museum in Paris. I pulled out the Rodin book. The cover was torn, there was a coffee ring on it, and when I cracked it open, the slippery pages smelled faintly like cigarettes.

I sat on the floor and thumbed through it. It was written in French. I could only understand bits of it, but the writing wasn't the point. The pictures were. *Don't think of Zack,* I told myself as I searched frantically for *The Kiss*. I found it and snapped the book shut, biting my lip. I bought it. It was a sign of some sort. I wasn't sure what it meant exactly, but I felt Nina next to me again, whispering about something I needed to understand, a place I needed to go and see, even if I had to wear Talbots khakis to get there.

A few hours later, I was twenty-seven minutes early for my first day of training, which was somehow worse than being late. I'd left the inn with plenty of time to spare in case something came up. I don't know what I thought was going to happen, but if I wanted to train for lacrosse and make eight thousand dollars in nine weeks, I had to stick to a schedule and not screw up. Every day I was going to eat three healthy meals, run five miles, and get eight hours of sleep. The busier I was, the less time I had to think about Zack and Parker.

When I arrived at the restaurant I had a nasty blister from my flats. I'd always thought of them as comfortable shoes. I'd considered wearing the Easy Spirits Mom had forced on me. I'd taken them out of my suitcase and tried them on and everything, but I couldn't. Not with the Talbots khakis. Liz told me I looked like I'd mugged a granny and run off with her trousers and trainers. The idea of pairing my granny pants with the Easy Spirits was too awful to think about, but as I hobbled into Breezes I knew I'd been wrong to prioritize beauty.

A bartender was checking bottle levels and making notes. He was facing the Nantucket Sound, jotting something on a form. The clouds had burned off and the late afternoon light was hazy gold. The plastic sheeting that had covered the windows was rolled up. A cool breeze rustled the pages of his notebook.

"Hey," I said. "Do you have any Band-Aids?"

He turned around as if to speak, but instead of telling me where the first-aid kit was, he let the moment hang in the air, waiting long enough for the blush on my cheeks to deepen to a fevered, stinging glow. It was Guitar Guy, leaning on the bar like he owned the place.

"Nice pants," he said with a wicked grin.

Fifteen

"SO YOU'RE THE NEW WAITRESS I'VE BEEN HEARING ABOUT," Guitar Guy said as he showed me through the bustling kitchen, alive with knives chopping and Spanish chatter, to a little locker room.

"I guess so," I said, wondering if one of these lockers was going to be mine, and if so, what I was supposed to keep in it. Guitar Guy opened a drawer in a metal cabinet, pulled out a first-aid kit, and handed me the Band-Aids. I took a few, sat down on the bench, and peeled one open. He sat next to me, leaning forward, forearms on knees. He smelled like herbs and spices, in a good way. I slipped off my shoes and applied the Band-Aids, oddly self-conscious.

"Hey, Ben, glad to see you're showing Cricket around," Karla said, appearing from around the corner. "Is the inventory done?"

"*Sí, el jefe,*" he said, and turned to me. "Cricket. Cool name."

"Nice to meet you, Ben."

This would have been the appropriate place to shake hands, but for some reason neither of us made a move, until at last, he tapped my elbow with his. I tapped his back reflexively. He smiled and tapped again, and so did I. What were we doing? A deep pink punished my cheeks. Karla tossed me an apron. I caught it and held it to my hot face for a second, hiding my blush.

"Well, at least we don't have to worry about you being a *brown*-noser," he said.

"Oh, you should worry," I said, peeking out from behind the apron. "Blue-nosers are the ones you have to watch out for."

I met the rest of the employees at the staff meal—chicken curry over rice. I sat at the communal table, determined to be my most charming self. There were three busboys, Hector, Steve, and Kevin; a few line cooks whose names I didn't catch; a tattooed dishwasher who grabbed some food and returned to the kitchen before I could introduce myself; and three other servers: Nicky, who spent winters skiing in Colorado and summers hanging out in Nantucket; James, a senior at Middlebury College; and Amy, who was tiny and beautiful, like a living doll. She had a thin tattoo—a simple line that encircled her arm like a bracelet—bright red lipstick, and long, mascaraed eyelashes under which her dark eyes flickered with intelligence.

"Do you know her?" Amy asked Ben, without acknowledging that the *her* was right there, sitting next to him.

"We met on the ferry," I said. "He touched my nose, like, out of nowhere!"

"That's weird," Amy said and stabbed a bit of chicken.

"Well, look at that nose," Ben said, gesturing to me. "It's a great nose." Amy reddened, her face almost matching her lipstick. I covered my nose with my hand as Ben's knee knocked mine.

"Cricket you'll be shadowing Amy," Karla said. "Stick to her like glue."

"Okay," I said. Amy pushed her chair from the table, grabbed her plate, walked away, and kicked open the kitchen door. I looked to Ben for help, but he was texting under the table.

"Get back here, Amy," Karla called. "We're about to go over the specials, *mija!*"

It didn't take long to learn my first lesson: following someone who doesn't want to be followed sucks.

"What are you doing?" I asked Amy as she punched a number into the computer.

"Uh, clocking in," she said.

"Do I clock in?"

"Not for training," Amy said, checking her text messages.

I didn't know if I was getting paid for the training and I didn't dare ask. About a half hour later, after Amy had prepped the coffee and tea station, checked the desserts, and memorized the specials, we got our first table. Our second was ten minutes later. And then our third, fourth, and fifth were sat all at once. Before I knew it, our whole section was full. I stood behind Amy as she greeted people, offered drinks, recited specials, answered questions, and took orders, all without writing anything down. I followed her as she wove through customers and staff, hustling back and forth from the bar, the tables, the kitchen, and the computer stations, never once checking to see if she'd lost me.

By around seven thirty p.m., our first tables were finishing their desserts, three others were working their way through their entrees, and the other two were relaxing over cocktails. Amy leaned against the computer stand and I hovered. She sighed and headed toward what I thought was the kitchen, so I followed.

"I'm going to the bathroom," Amy said. "Get lost!"

"Sorry," I said and slinked back out to what I now had learned was the "floor."

Ben laughed at me from behind the bar.

"I'm supposed to follow her everywhere," I said and shrugged.

"She's in a bad mood," Ben said with a smile as he poured a glass of chardonnay, two red wines, and a gin and tonic.

"Do you have anything to do with that?" I asked, and for the first time he looked a little sad.

"Just drop these on table five for her, okay?"

"Um, which one is that?"

"The fifth one in from the door on the left."

"Hey, do you know if I get paid for tonight?" I asked, picking up the tray with both hands. I wasn't ready for a one-handed carry. Would I ever be?

"Minimum wage. Unless Amy decides to share her tips."

Minimum wage, I thought, and counted aloud to find table number five.

Right after I delivered the drinks, Karla told me I could go home for the night. "Same thing tomorrow. Wednesday you'll learn how to close."

"So I did okay?"

"You did great."

"Um, did you find out about the housing?"

"We'll put you out on Surfside Road. I'm sure we can squeeze another bed in there somehow. I think Amy has the double bed. She'll roll over for you."

"Oh, okay." Was she serious? The idea of sharing a bed with Amy sent the taste of chicken curry to the back of my throat. Amy was leaning on the bar, one foot kicking up behind her, whispering something to Ben. What sort of lipstick did she use that stayed on so perfectly like that?

"And it's a hundred and fifty each week out of your paycheck," Karla said. "For the housing."

"Sounds good," I said, though that seemed like a lot if I was going to be sharing a bed with someone who hated me.

"Cricket," Amy called. I turned. It was the first time she'd said my name even though we'd been tethered by an invisible rope for several hours. She draped a proprietary arm around Ben and pointed to my apron. "Are you taking that home for a souvenir?"

"Oh, whoops," I said. As I unknotted the coffee-stained apron and headed to the locker room I heard her say to Ben, "What kind of a name is Cricket, anyway?"

I practically crawled out of the restaurant. Several hours of waitressing had tired me out more than a whole lacrosse tournament. My blistered feet hurt even as I walked on the outside of the folded-in heels of my flats. My neck felt like it'd been stepped on, and I knew that I smelled like onion rings. I paused on Main Street, about to head into the pharmacy for an ice-cream sandwich, when I decided to go to Mitchell's Book Corner instead. Seeing my name in George Gust's book never failed to give me a little boost, and it was even better if I saw it in the actual store rather than in my own personal copy. I had one foot in the store when I spotted Zack straight ahead. *Zack!*

Don't care, I commanded myself as I silently stepped back to the sidewalk and slinked behind a tree. I steadied myself, tilted my head, breathed bark. There was the boy I knew in a baseball cap, bent over a book, turning the pages with care. He shifted his weight and turned ninety degrees, revealing the cover of the book. It was the reissued edition of her collected works, the one with the bright blue cover that my English teacher constantly praised. Emily Dickinson was what I had been reading on the beach last summer when we spent our first day alone together. Emily Dickinson was the book that held open the window he climbed into to find me. "Emily Dickinson was an American genius," I'd told him once, and we'd both burst into laughter because I'd sounded so serious. Emily Dickinson!

It was a sign. He was thinking about me. This Parker relationship was some kind of misguided illusion, some terrible strain of boarding school amnesia. I couldn't see him now, not in my Talbots khakis, not when I smelled like garlic and onions, with coffee grounds under my fingernails. I stepped out of my shoes and ran back to the inn barefoot, this new information filling me with lightness and speed.

When I got back to the manager's apartment, I took a long shower. The food smell lifted from my hair and skin after the third scrubbing. I slathered myself with lotion, put on my Brown lacrosse T-shirt, and climbed into my makeshift bed on the sofa. I heard mumbles from Liz's room. She was probably on the phone with Shane, who was out on the Cape for at least another few days.

From the window, sounds of kids laughing drifted up with the scent of honeysuckle and freshly mowed grass. I pulled out the *Musée de Rodin* book and looked at *The Kiss*. I closed my eyes and let myself slip, remembering the first time Zack and I had spent the whole night together. I gave myself the dream like a gift, like a stolen bar of chocolate.

Sixteen

"DO YOU SUPPOSE THAT'S YOUR LITTLE, UM, CORNER?" LIZ asked and pointed to a bare twin-size mattress with a tiny pillow on it on the floor. Liz said it was the kind that you got on an airplane for international flights. The mattress was one of five in a room meant for two, three of which were on actual bed frames and two of which lay on the stained carpet. The one without the sheets on it was definitely meant for me. I just knew it. "At least you won't be sharing a bed with Amy," Liz said.

It was four days later and even though I'd been prepared, I had yet to run into Zack or Jules. I certainly wasn't going to run into them out here. Liz and I were at the staff house out on Surfside Road. It was a tiny one-bedroom, one-bathroom shack that I was going to be sharing with six girls, one of whom was snoring in a thong and T-shirt, facedown on the futon in the living room in front of a TV tuned to a daytime talk show, advising as to how to "shop your own closet." The box of wine on the coffee table indicated she'd spent the previous night like this, too. I didn't recognize her, at least not from this angle, so she must have been one of the girls from the Wamp.

Inside the bedroom, only one of the beds was made. It was probably the one belonging to Nicky, the career waitress. The other beds, littered with magazines, with sheets and clothes strewn everywhere, made it look as if zombies had attacked without warning.

"And at least you're near the window?" Liz said.

"Yeah." I stepped over an empty beer bottle and an open bag of hot Cheetos and looked out the window. It was open a crack, but needed to be up all the way all the time. It smelled like a mixture of old cheese and socks in there. There was a tang to the odor that was more taste than smell. People think girls are neat and clean and boys are the messy ones, but this house was living proof that that wasn't true. I opened the screenless window and stuck my head out. Amy was in the yard reading the *New York Times*. No lipstick.

In the last few days she'd learned to tolerate having me follow her around, as long as I didn't talk too much, and I'd learned to pick up whatever I could through observation alone, since she was not about to provide instruction. If I had any questions, Nicky was the one who'd give answers. I'd also learned not to talk to Ben in front of Amy; whatever they had going on was complicated and semisecret, and she did her best to limit my time at the bar. If there were drinks to pick up, she sent me to fold napkins, wipe up the dessert station, or check on appetizers in the kitchen.

"It's not so terrible," Liz said, peering out the window to the patch of dry grass behind the house where Amy was now lighting a cigarette. "Look, there's a backyard for lacrosse practice."

"Yeah," I said, imagining practicing shots on goal over a smoking, sunbathing Amy. So far, I'd kept up with my running, but I hadn't done my stick drills at all. Amy turned around and squinted at the sound of our voices.

"Hi," I smiled too big and waved too cheerfully.

"Oh," she muttered, turned back to her newspaper, and crossed her legs. Amy had the toned legs of a dancer. She really was beautiful.

"Twat," Liz said too loudly. She pulled back from the window, and took another look around. "I'm just going to use the loo, and then I'll leave you to get settled."

I pursed my lips and nodded. I wanted to throw myself at her feet, cling to her, and beg her not to leave me there. I sat on the lumpy mattress and tried not to cry. A line of ants crawled up the wall and toward the window. If Zack and I did get back together, there was no way I wanted him climbing through this window.

I took a deep breath and searched for some empty space in a closet, but the one in the bedroom was claimed. The bar was bending under the weight of crowded, overloaded hangers. On the floor were a jumble of shoes, and two full hampers. This was one closet I did not want to shop. I shut the door as if the organisms living in the teeming piles of dirty laundry might attack.

Maybe there was another closet in the living room? Doing my best not to disturb Thonged Snoring Girl, I grasped at the first doorknob I found, but it was on the door to the bathroom. Liz was standing in front of the sink washing her hands with a vigor I'd never seen.

"It's awful," I said.

"A hovel!" Liz said. "Look." She gestured at the toilet with its nasty, rust-colored ring. Pinching together her thumb and forefinger, she opened the flimsy, ripped shower curtain to reveal a plastic stall with blackish mold blossoming in all the corners. Liz washed her hands again and then looked around for something to dry them on. She paused centimeters shy of the mildewed towels that were piled on top of one another on a single hook. Holding her breath, she dried her hands on her jeans.

"I'll scrub it myself," I said. "I'll just get some rubber gloves and some Ajax and roll up my sleeves and do it."

"Have you seen the kitchen yet?"

I shook my head.

Liz swallowed. "You can stay with me for one more night, two maximum, but you have to make yourself very scarce. It's the first night Shane is back from the Cape, and I do not want to be disturbed."

"I'll hang out in the kitchen until you text me that the coast is clear."

"It might not be until very, very late. We're sexually adventurous."

"I know. I don't care. I'll sleep outdoors in the hammock if you want."

"Let's get out of here," she said. "Quick, before we contract athlete's foot." She pointed to a stagnant puddle in the shower where a mosquito hovered lasciviously. "Or dengue fever."

We grabbed my stuff.

"Who are you?" Thonged Snoring Girl asked, groggy, wiping her crusty eyes with clumsy hands.

"Figments of your imagination," Liz said as we flew out the door. "Mere shadows."

"Hey, can you drop these on table nine?" Ben asked that night as I passed by the bar on my way to see how the customers at table sixteen were doing with their appetizers. It was my last night of training and I was pretty much a free girl. I'd managed five tables on my own, from the Lillet aperitifs to the beach plum sorbet. It killed me that Amy was going to get all the tips. Ben was chilling martini glasses, lining up highballs, and tearing off tickets all at the same time, but with such laid-back summer style, he didn't even look like he was working. "Amy's in the weeds."

"Sure," I said, noticing the appealing line of his side as he reached for a wineglass. He opened a fresh bottle of Pouilly-Fumé, ran a blade below the lower ridge to remove the wrapper, twisted the corkscrew with a confident wrist, and poured two cool, pale, straw-colored glasses with the kind of relaxed competence that made watching him so easy. "And I know exactly where table nine is."

"I'm starting to see why you got into Brown," he said, and, without breaking eye contact, placed the drinks on a tray. "You should come by the brewery tomorrow, I'm playing some new songs. I've been meaning to ask you for a few days, but it's hard to get you alone."

"Oh," I said. *Was he asking me out?*

"Everyone's invited," he said.

"Fuck," Amy said under her breath as she punched an order into a nearby computer and messed up. "Fuck me." She canceled the order, blinked her long, luxurious lashes, and started again. "Hey, are you moving into the Surfside house, or what?"

"Tomorrow," I said.

"Just so you know, I get the first shower in the morning."

"Okay," I said, too cheerful, as always. I was probably always going to be too cheerful for grumpy alternative girls. I sighed. She marched off.

Ben waited until Amy was in the kitchen, and then he leaned a little closer. He smelled like a man. Herbs and spices. Gin and lime. Summer and salt. "Before the show I'm going surfing. Want to come?"

"I don't surf," I said. Not only was I certain that Amy would suffocate me with my own pillow in my sleep if I went surfing with Ben, I was so focused on seeing Zack I didn't think I'd be able to concentrate on another activity.

It had been almost a week since I'd seen him at Mitchell's Book Corner, and even though I'd been hanging out in town on my mornings off, always ready, always in cute outfits, I had yet to run into him again.

"I can teach you," he said.

"I think I have plans," I said.

"Okay," Ben said, biting his lip. "You sure about that?"

I nodded, turning away. Again with the blushing! I was going to have to start wearing ski masks to work so I could hide, even as my cheeks betrayed me. It was like my face had its own relationship with him.

"Okay, no pressure." He seemed to mean it, like he wasn't disappointed at all, and I was considering changing my mind as he handed me the tray of drinks. It was heavier than I'd expected. "If you look at them, you'll spill. Don't look."

"I got it," I said. I steadied my gaze on my destination: table nine. I knew Ben was watching, and I was determined to deliver the drinks without spilling a drop. But when I stepped out on the porch and their faces came into view, I almost lost the drinks, my footing, my breath, and my mind.

It was the Claytons.

Seventeen

"CRICKET!" JULES SAID AS I ARRIVED AT THE TABLE SHAKING so hard that I had to put the tray down in front of her. It was Jules, Mr. Clayton, Zack, and one empty chair. Mom had been right about the Easy Spirits. Work had been a lot more comfortable once I'd surrendered, but seeing Zack in nursing home shoes made me want to crawl under the table, out of the restaurant, and down the beach, and swim home to Providence. I swallowed, not sure I had enough saliva to speak. I'd wanted to see him. I'd dreamed about it, but not like this.

"Surprise," I said and laughed weakly. "Again?"

"Hi." Zack said. He held me with his eyes. For a second, it was just us. This was no high five. For a moment, I thought he was going to stand up and kiss me in front of Amy and Ben and Jules and everyone.

"Hi," I said. His cheeks patched with red.

"Cricket Elizabeth Thompson," Jules said. "*Sérieusement?* What are you doing here? What happened to Leo's?"

"It's kind of a long story." I handed a Coke to Jules. "And I've been meaning to call you, but I just kept, I don't know, not doing it." I was about to give Zack his Coke, but my hand was trembling so much that I had to put the glass down.

"I got it," Zack said, leaning over and taking it. His pinkie brushed the back of my hand. I willed my blood to slow its pace.

"Hi, Mr. Clayton," I said.

"It's great to see you," Mr. Clayton said. "I'm glad you're working here. This means we'll be seeing a lot of you this summer."

"We joined the Wamp!" Jules said. "We finally got in off the waiting list!"

"After fifteen years," Mr. Clayton said, laughing and pushing his Prada glasses up the bridge of his nose.

"Yes," Jules said, making pointed eye contact with Mr. Clayton. "Because of Mom. It's what Mom wanted."

"Jules, can we just enjoy the night?" Mr. Clayton asked. Zack stared into his Coke and stirred it with the cocktail straw.

"Well, I think it's great. Here's your wine." I handed Mr. Clayton his Pouilly-Fumé, which left me with one more glass. I looked at the empty seat. Who was it for? Oh, god, I thought, did seventeen-year-old Parker have the gall to order wine? I watched Jules frown as a pretty woman in a hot-pink minidress sat in the remaining seat. I placed the wine in front of her.

"This is my friend, Jennifer," Mr. Clayton said. I heard the quotation marks snap into place around the word *friend*. "Jennifer, this is Cricket."

"Cricket, what a cute name!" Jennifer said. "I'm so very pleased to meet you."

"You, too," I said. I felt a hand on my back. A strong, tiny hand. It was Amy. She cleared her throat and gestured for me to step aside.

"I'm Amy, and I'll be your server tonight. Any questions about the menu?"

"We need a few minutes, right, guys?" Mr. Clayton said.

"Are the moules-frites good?" Zack asked.

"The best. Our chef brought the recipe back from Paris," Amy said.

"That's what I'm having," Zack said and shut his menu.

"Aw, because of Parker?" Jennifer mewled. "How cute is that, y'all? His girl is in Paris, so he's ordering French food!"

His girl?

"Is that right?" asked Amy in her fake waitress voice. "That *is* romantic."

Paris? The Paris I'd been reading about in my *Musée de Rodin* book?

"Not really," Zack said. "My girlfriend is in Paris, but I just feel like mussels."

Girlfriend. The way he tossed off the word felt like a rock through my window.

"What's she doing there?" I asked, too loud, too serious.

Amy glared at me from under her mascaraed eyelashes. "Uh, don't mind Cricket, she's training. We're not sure she's going to last."

"We know her." Jules eyed Amy, ready to throw a punch.

"She's like family," Mr. Clayton added. I wanted to send him a thank-you note.

"Parker's studying in Paris," Zack said to me.

"Right!" Jules rolled her eyes. "She's 'studying.' Puh-leez."

"Jules," Zack began, but I couldn't hang around for another word.

I backed away from the table and wove through the restaurant to the ladies' room, still carrying that stupid tray. I looked in the mirror and splashed cold water on my face. *Don't cry,* I told my reflection. *Don't you dare cry!* I patted my face dry with one of the cloth-quality paper towels and opened the door, where I found myself inches from Zack, who was headed to the men's room.

"I don't understand," I blurted out before I could stop myself, knowing even as the words were leaving my mouth that I would regret them later. "Why are you with her?"

"I called you," he said, looking almost scared. "Remember? And you told me it was over."

"What?" Anger, quick as lightning, flashed through me. "*THAT's* how you interpreted that phone call?" I uncurled my fists, took a deep breath. "I didn't think . . . Zack, I had no friends at school. I was trying to get my life back. I told you to wait! If you interpreted it like that it's because you wanted to!"

"I needed you. And you weren't there."

"What? No." I reached out to take his hand.

He squeezed it quickly and let go. "Yes, Cricket."

It was like the high five, part two. "But Parker? *Parker?* Are you fucking kidding me?"

"Hey," he said, giving me a stop-sign hand. "Hey."

"You're going to stay with her?" I asked. I was on a roll.

"You don't know her or—"

"Oh, I know enough," I said. Amy was walking toward me, looking super pissed off, but I couldn't deal with her right now. "What I don't know is why you read Emily Dickinson in your spare time."

"What are you talking about?" He flushed, bright as one of the buoys bobbing in the harbor.

Amy grabbed me by the apron and pulled me into the hot kitchen. I'd learned on the lacrosse field that some of those tiny girls sure are strong.

"What the hell was that? If I get a shitty tip, I swear, you are going down."

"This isn't about your tip, Amy," I said as I retied my apron. One of the cooks licked his lips as he watched us. I turned my back to the kitchen and lowered my voice. "And it's not like you've been giving me any actual training."

"You want training? Okay. You spent way too long at that table, even if you do know them. Table six doesn't even have menus yet. Your shirt is untucked in the back. Two days ago you ate a pastry within sight of the floor. That's enough for some of these dickheads to refuse to pay their bill. And you should never, never put a tray on the table like you just did. If Karla sees you do that, she'll fire you like this." She snapped her fingers.

"Thanks for the help," I said, not sure myself if I was being serious or sarcastic. Then I kicked open the door and walked straight to the bar.

Ben took one look at me, poured me a Coke, and pushed it toward me. It was sweet and soothing. Maybe I was done with high school boys. Maybe all this blushing in front of Ben was because my nervous system knew what was up. "How do you get to the brewery?"

"It's on the way to Cisco," he said, grinning. "Why, you're gonna come?"

I wrote my number on a napkin. "Text me the address."

"What about surfing?" he asked.

"I'll think about it," I said.

"Oh, you're going to come surfing with me," he said as he entered my number into his phone. "And you're going to love it."

"Hey, Cricket," Amy snapped as she walked by. "Table six?"

Eighteen

I SHOULD HAVE KNOWN BETTER, I TOLD MYSELF AS I HEADED home that night. I was like a lobster that had willingly jumped into the pot. What was I thinking? After the high five, it had been clear that Zack and I were through. How could he have misunderstood me on the phone before Thanksgiving? I'd told him I loved him. But that's what happened when people did long distance, right? Love got lost in translation, scrambled at the cell-phone towers, twisted in the wireless wind. I'd tried so hard to avoid it, but it'd happened anyway.

Who knows why he was reading Emily Dickinson? Maybe it was for school. Maybe it was pure, unemotional, intellectual curiosity. Maybe I had dreamed up the moment, because I wanted it to exist. A Jeep full of college dudes blasted by, blaring ghetto rap and emitting such high levels of testosterone it was a wonder I didn't sprout a pair of balls from proximity. As Amy would say, they were FAAs (pronounced *fahs*), Future Assholes of America. Amy probably thought Zack was a FAA, which of course, he wasn't.

Or was he? I mean, he was dating Parker. *Parker*. I shook my head. It didn't make sense. I walked past the Nantucket Yacht Club, where sounds of a wedding band playing "I Heard It Through the Grapevine" blew in on a harbor breeze. I wished someone would tell me through the grapevine what he saw in her. Though it made me snarl, I tried to list her good qualities just so I could understand.

Okay, so Parker had awesome hair. That much could not be denied. She was bold, in her way. She had a number of horse-related achievements. She was a senator's daughter, rich, exposed to music and art, well traveled, well dressed. I stood still for a moment, wondering if this made her better than me in Zack's eyes. Did all those first-class tickets to the wonders of the world, all those two-hundred-dollar jeans and skillful descents of double black diamond trails distinguish her from me in a way I couldn't even see?

I turned up Main Street. My pace quickened. Was she, like, really elegant or something and I didn't even realize it? Impossible, I thought. No one was more elegant than Nina, and Parker was nothing like Nina. But was I like Nina? It's not like I could do the things on Nina's life list the way Parker could. I couldn't go to Paris, not until it was time for my junior year abroad, anyway. As I climbed the stairs to the manager's apartment, I felt that dagger of panic. How was I supposed to do everything, be everything? I'd done the best I could in high school, run myself ragged, but suddenly that wasn't enough. The rules had changed and I didn't even know what they were.

That was when I noticed that the shades weren't drawn in the manager's apartment. Liz was supposed to be having her wild sex marathon with Shane, and I was under strict instructions to insert cotton balls in my ears and head straight to the sofa. But all the lights were on. I could see directly into the bedroom. It was empty. Liz was in the kitchen, pacing with a bottle of wine. Not a glass, a bottle.

"Liz, are you okay?" I asked, barging in. She burst into tears.

"What happened?" I'd never seen Liz cry. I'd never even imagined it, but she was shaking and sobbing. I put my arms around her.

"He dumped me," she said, gasping for breath. "He was seeing someone else this whole time!"

"Oh, Liz," I said, guiding her to the sofa and handing her a box of tissues. "Are you sure?"

"Am I sure?" she slurred. She flung an arm in what I guessed was the general direction of Shane. "I saw the bastard with my own eyes."

"How? Where?" I ran to the sink and poured her a glass of water, but she reached for the wine again.

"He called to cancel our date, said he needed one more day on the Cape."

"That doesn't necessarily mean anything." I handed her the water again.

"I just had this weird feeling that he wasn't actually on the Cape. Like, it was weird. Paranormal. A sixth sense. I drove by his house."

"Uh-oh."

"He was out on the porch, kissing another girl." Her face screwed up. "Svetlana. Skinny, horrible Svetlana. Svetlana the cow!"

"No!"

"Normally, I'm like, stiff upper lip, but, Cricket?" She waved her hand as another rush of tears came on. "I thought we were going to get married. I didn't go to university." She gripped my shoulders, eyes round with fear. "I didn't go to university."

"You still can."

"Where?"

"I don't know, but you can."

"I've got to start my applications." She tripped as she reached toward her laptop. "University!"

"Why don't we tackle that tomorrow?" I guided her toward the bedroom and turned down her perfectly made bed, which was scattered with rose petals and surrounded by unlit candles. I swept my arm across the coverlet, sending the rose petals to the floor. "What do you say we get you to bed?"

"I can't," Liz said as she crawled under the covers. She looked like a little kid, the sheets pulled up to her nose, her curls fanned out on the pillow. "Then I'll have to get up. And if I get up, it will all be real."

"You just sleep. I'll set up tomorrow," I said, as I sat on the edge of the bed.

"The muffins and everything?"

"The muffins and everything." I got up and backed away and turned off the light.

"Don't go," Liz said. "Don't leave me alone tonight."

"Okay," I lay down next to her. I spotted a tube of some kind of sex oil and gingerly knocked it under the bed and out of sight.

"Tell me a story," she said, flipping the pillow over.

"Once upon a time, there was a frog."

"Was he actually a prince?" she asked.

"Nope, just a frog," I said, making it up as I went along. "A girl frog. And she had many, many adventures."

The frog had moved to a lovely new pond, gained employment with an alligator, learned to play the banjo, and entertained a flock of fairies before Liz finally started snoring.

Nineteen

"YOU JUST LET ME HANDLE GETTING US THE DRINKS," LIZ
said the next afternoon. We were at the brewery, which was
in the middle of the island, near Bartlett's Farm. It was
made up of a cluster of small buildings, each one with a
little bar inside it. One served beer, one served wine, and the
third served vodka drinks. In the middle was a courtyard
with picnic tables, crowded with people in sundresses and
flip-flops. Someone was grilling hamburgers in the parking
lot and selling them for a mere five bucks, which was way
below the going Nantucket rate of eighteen.

"I'm not drinking, because I have to practice, remember?" I said, even though I knew Liz wouldn't listen. She
hadn't surfaced until almost noon. I'd made the coffee and
muffins at five a.m., handled the checkouts, and canceled

my date with Ben in order to greet any early new arrivals. I'd been planning on working out that afternoon, but I made the mistake of telling Liz that Ben, the bartender I'd met on the ferry, was playing at the brewery, and she'd said the only cure for her horribly broken heart was cranberry vodka, a good crowd, and the company of a loyal friend. "Please," she'd said, her curls tossed and messy. "Please come with me." So there I was, putting off my lacrosse practice yet again.

"Besides," I added, scoping out the small stage where Ben would soon be playing, "we don't have ID."

"I know everyone who works here," Liz said. "Get us a couple of hamburgers and find us a seat up front."

I had just paid for the burgers and found a picnic bench in the shade when I saw Karla. It was pretty much impossible to miss her blue hair. She had her arm around a petite woman with coffee-colored skin and dangly earrings. She waved just as Liz returned with two cranberry drinks.

"It's Karla," I said, watching my boss approach, a cold, alcoholic drink in my hand. "She knows I'm not twenty-one."

"When are you going to realize that you don't have to be such a very good girl?" Liz said. I thought this was a little harsh after I'd improvised a thirty-minute frog story for her the night before.

"Hi, Karla," I said, hiding the drink behind my back as she introduced me to her girlfriend, Marie.

"Heard about Shane," Karla said to Liz. "What a jerk. Did he really think he could get away with it on this island?"

"I'd rather not discuss it," Liz said and gulped her drink, shaking the ice at the bottom.

"Marie, this is Cricket, my newest waitress," Karla said, introducing me to her girlfriend. "Amy trained her all week and she's ready to bust out on her own."

"Hey, there," Marie said, and then laughed a little. "How did your niece feel about training a cute blond?"

"Your niece?" I asked.

"Oh, Karla, look, it's Lisa. I've got to talk to her about the garden tour before Annabelle Burke does," Marie said.

"Gotta run," Karla said. "And hey, when are you moving into the Surfside house?"

"She's not," Liz said before I could answer. "She's living with me."

"Okay, see ya," Karla said. She pointed to my cup and added, "Don't get caught with that drink."

"Liz, are you sure?" I asked, handing the rest of my drink to her. She handed it back.

"'Course I'm sure. I'm not one of those girls who likes to be alone."

"Thank you!" I said. "That's so awesome of you. Seriously."

"Is that your bartender?" Liz asked, not letting me fuss. I turned to see Ben step onstage with his guitar. "This better not be a love song. I'm not drunk enough."

Ben began to strum. It was a love song. His voice was low and kind of country. It was a little rough, so that even though he was singing quietly about the moon, it had grit.

I was just starting to melt into his voice when I saw Amy swaying to the music, front and center, gazing at him like he was a rock star.

"I can't tell if they're dating," I said to Liz, motioning to Amy. "But she's definitely—"

"Fucking him," Liz said with a full mouth.

"I was going to say 'in love.' Check out the way she's looking at him." Amy's head was tilted. Her eyes were focused and soft with emotion. For the first time, she looked sweet.

"She may be looking at him," Liz said, "but he can't take his eyes off of you."

Twenty

I WAS IN THE WALK-IN FRIDGE AT BREEZES, STANDING ON my tiptoes and reaching for a fresh container of nonfat milk so I could stock the coffee station (nonfat milk is a lot easier to foam than whole), when I felt a sharp, searing pain in my neck. I gasped and clutched the place where my shoulder met my neck on the right side and which was now tight and throbbing. *Ouch.* My whole body contracted and curled. I was bent over, eyes squeezed shut, seeing yellow spots, when I felt a sure, calm hand on my back.

"Breathe."

It was Ben.

"My neck," I said, sucking refrigerator air in through my teeth.

"It's probably just a muscle spasm," Ben said, guiding me to a milk crate.

"It really hurts," I said, sitting down on the crate.

"It's tension. You need to relax."

It was true. I was exhausted from seven consecutive days of waitressing, early mornings covering for Liz, and squeezing in lacrosse practice whenever I could, which had only been twice. My plan was working. I'd only been waitressing for a week, and I'd already made a thousand dollars—but as another flash of pain struck, I knew it was time for a break.

"I got ya," Ben said, pulling up another milk crate and sitting behind me. "Let go of your shoulder."

"I can't." I was afraid if I let go, the pain would spread.

"Breathe with me."

I took a deep breath in and he rested his callused guitar hands on my shoulders, pressing his thumbs into my neck. We breathed together a few times.

"Oh," I said. "Oh." The pain changed color, broke apart. I risked turning my head. "Ouch!"

"Just focus on what's right in front of you."

"Mayonnaise," I said, looking up at a wall of industrial-size jars of condiments. Ben laughed, and I could feel it in his hands as he continued to knead my shoulders.

"How's it now?"

"Still pretty bad," I said. Even though the pain had dissipated, I didn't want him to stop.

"I know what you need. You need some time on the ocean. You want to go surfing tomorrow?"

"Yes," I said, glad he couldn't see me smiling. Neither of us had talked about our surfing date since the morning I'd canceled. I kept waiting for him to bring it up, but he hadn't. Maybe he was waiting for me to bring it up. We were in some kind of standoff, and my interest in the date had risen an additional ten percent every day it went unmentioned. I had reserved tomorrow afternoon for running and going over lacrosse drills, but surfing was a form of exercise, wasn't it?

"You're so tense you're like a shrinky dink," he said just as the door was flung open.

"What the hell is going on in here?" Karla asked.

Ben lifted his hands. I instantly missed them. They were experts, those hands.

"I had a muscle spasm," I said. "Ben was helping me."

"I'm sure he was," Karla said. Her glare scared me. Authority figures rarely looked at me with anything other than affection or relief. Her eyes were full of accusation. "You guys know my policy about staff relationships, right? You get into one, you're outta here."

"Um, I actually didn't know that policy," I said, standing up, no problem. My neck was miraculously healed.

"Karla," Ben said, cool as a gimlet. He pulled a carton of milk from the high shelf and handed it to me. "I walked in here and she was doubled over in pain."

"Well, just don't make me call you into my office, okay? Ben, you of all people should know better, and that bar's not going to prep itself. Cricket, you have a visitor."

"I do?" I took my milk and headed to the floor. My heart pirouetted. For a second, I thought it might be Zack.

It was Jules, in her black bikini and paisley cover-up, all long legs, highlights, and freckles. I felt a kick of disappointment. Would I ever learn? She helped herself to a couple of olives from the bar and asked, "What happened to you?"

"What do you mean?" I nodded toward a table where a stack of napkins awaited folding.

"You're all flushed and flustered and shit."

I shook my head and waved my hand, like, *Oh, nothing*, but I must've glanced at Ben without realizing it, because Jules took him in, his magic hands full of lemons, and cocked an eyebrow. I shrugged. She grinned.

"Well," she said, folding her slender hands on the table as we sat down. "I'm here for a few reasons. There's something about Parker—"

"Jules, I can't even . . ." I trailed off as Jules knocked some sand off her foot onto the floor. Karla had warned us that club members acted like they owned this place. *And that's good*, she'd said. *That's how they're supposed to feel.* Still, I had to bite my cheek to stop myself from making a face. I'd swept that floor twenty minutes ago. I peeled a napkin from the stack and started folding. "I don't want to hear about them."

"It's just that, well, it's complicated," Jules said.

"Yeah, you've both told me."

"And, like, so stereotypical."

"I don't want to know," I said. The last thing I wanted was a whiff of hope. I'd volunteered to take the indoor section every night, the one nearest the entrance. It was the least desirable. The big spenders all wanted to sit on the porch or the patio, but I was willing to take the less lucrative section if it meant I didn't have to risk seeing Zack and Parker frolicking on the beach.

"Okay," Jules sighed. "If you say so. Do you want to go to the beach tomorrow?"

"I'm going surfing," I said, and I nodded in Ben's direction.

"How old is he?" she mouthed.

Twenty-two, I mouthed back.

"Then the next day," she said, standing and tossing her bag over her shoulder. "We'll have lots to talk about. Meet me at the club at noon."

"Will they let me in?"

"Of course." Her laugh was as sunny as her freckled face. Never had she looked so pretty. Never had she sounded more grown-up. "Just tell them you're with me."

Twenty-one

FROM FAR AWAY, SURFING LOOKED LIKE A GRACEFUL activity, but now that I'd lugged the long, unwieldy board over the sand and was paddling ineffectively, Ben pushing me from behind, it didn't feel elegant or smooth. Cisco was a different beach from Jetties or Steps. It was on the ocean side, and I realized that what I'd sometimes been calling the ocean at Steps wasn't the ocean at all. It was the Nantucket Sound, protected and sheltered. Out here, on the southern side of the island, the waves were big. You could feel them rolling in with power and force, pushed from a wild place.

I was lying on the surfboard just like Ben had showed me when he'd given me a little lesson on the sand. We were headed out to beyond where the waves broke. We weren't even surfing yet, but it was already hard. A big wave, one that

I wouldn't have attempted to body surf, was coming right at us. "Point the nose straight ahead," he said, swimming right behind. Water crashed over me and filled my nose and mouth. I held on tight to the board, even as my body lifted and slammed back down again. I'd always thought of myself as so courageous, but I felt small. Tiny even. I coughed saltwater.

"You okay?" he asked when we finally got to the place where the water rolled, soft and lilting. Ben held onto the board and shook his hair from his face.

"I'm fine," I said, even though I wanted to turn around.

"That was kind of big," he said, "but don't worry. Once you get up, you're going to love it. It's all about trusting the unknown."

I nodded as if I totally got it, wishing we could just stay right there, drifting and floating in the sun.

"So, what's going on with you and Amy?"

He sighed. "Nothing." I raised my eyebrows. "Not any-more. We were together, but it didn't work out. She's looking for something I just can't give." He shifted so that his torso rested on the board.

"I have this weird feeling she's really smart. Besides, I think she really likes you. You sound a little insensitive, you know." I splashed him. He didn't splash back.

"I came to Nantucket to get away from a complicated situation, not to get back into one."

"What do you mean?" The afternoon sun was strong. It pressed on my back. "What was your situation?"

"I was engaged," he said, looking away.

"Really?" *I was old enough to know someone who could be engaged?* "Like, to be married?"

"Yes," he said with a sad laugh. "We broke up in April."

His face shifted into an expression that seemed ancient. Even though I barely knew him, I imagined that his father and grandfather and great-grandfather had also looked like this at certain moments in their lives.

I scooted up on the surfboard. "What happened?"

"She cheated on me."

"Oh, I'm sorry."

He squinted, looking out in the distance. "Okay, a set is coming, are you ready?"

"I guess. Listen, I'm sorry if I brought up—"

"No worries. So, it's going to be just like I showed you on the beach." He turned the board around, pointing it toward the shore. "You're going to paddle, paddle, paddle, and when I say 'pop,' you hop up on your feet. Super fast."

"How will I know if it's the right time to pop?"

"I'll tell you," he said, and I was off. He was pushing me and I was paddling, paddling, paddling. "Pop!"

I tried to stand but hesitated, and when my body froze up, I fell off. I hit the surface and the wave swallowed me. Salt stung my throat as I tumbled, inhaling water. I spat it out as my head popped up, gasping. The leash that tethered me to the board tugged on my ankle, yanking me forward, and I was back under, feeling sand and pebbles and water spinning, churning over me. When I tried to break through the surface again, the board swung back and hit me in the ribs. A second wave rolled in and dragged me backward by the waist.

Stay calm, I told myself, *relax.* And calling up ancient information from some long-ago swimming class at the Providence YMCA, I allowed my body to move with the water instead of against it. Finally I felt the sand under my feet. I stood up and took big swallows of air. I held on to the board and let a smaller wave push me toward the beach.

By the time I was in the surf, Ben had caught up. "Hey, you okay?"

"I think I'm done," I said. I reached down and pulled the Velcro leash off, stumbling as another wave frothed around my legs. Ben carried the board to the beach.

"The good news is you look okay," he said, gazing into my eyes with a soft smile. "A little scared, but okay. We can try some smaller, gentler waves if you want."

I didn't want smaller waves. I didn't want gentler waves. I didn't want any waves. My inner forearms were raw and chafed from holding on to the board so tightly. I was out of breath. I was on the brink of tears. My ribs hurt.

"I'm going to rest," I said and peeled off the girls' wet suit lent to him by some surfer friend of his. I didn't even care what my bathing suit looked like or that I could feel the bottoms riding up my butt. I shook out the towel I'd bought from the thrift store and sat down on the warm, solid sand.

"You sure you're okay?" He crouched next to me.

"Yes," I said, digging my heels into the sand. I didn't want to let on how shaken up I was. I wasn't used to being physically scared or intimidated. I laid a cold hand over my left rib, where I felt the beginnings of a bruise. "You go ahead. I'll watch. Really, I'm fine." His eyes met mine. I wanted a few minutes alone. I put some confidence behind my shaky voice and a reassuring smile on my face. "I swear. I've just had a long week."

He went. A few minutes later, after I'd shaken the water from my ears, I watched him surf. He paddled and popped and rode. I stood up to get a better look. Usually Ben had his watchful spot from behind the bar and I was in his view as I waitressed. But now I was the watcher. I placed one hand on my forehead like a visor and the other on my aching side. Ben wasn't in a wet suit, so I could see the strength of his legs, the power of his core, and the beauty in his balance. His body was both familiar and foreign. He was a living Rodin. *The Walking Man. The Thinker. Saint John the Baptist.* He was all of them, but not made of marble, stuck in a museum in Paris. He was in motion. He was alive in the Atlantic.

I thought about Nina's list, and a great idea came to me, the kind that feels like opening a window. I didn't need Parker's money or connections. Screw that. I could live Nina's list, here on Nantucket. I could follow it and see where it led me. *Rodin is at Cisco,* I thought. *I don't need to go anywhere. I just need to open my eyes.*

A few good waves were Ben's medicine, because an hour later, when he emerged from the water with his board under his arm, he had that wicked grin on his face. And as the late afternoon sun caught the drops of water that slipped down his skin, he was actually sparkling.

Ben's car was an army green Land Rover from the 1970s with a canvas top that rolled up in the back. It belonged to his grandmother Sadie, whom he described as Joni Mitchell meets Rosie the Riveter. He was staying with her for the summer. I changed in the back, under the tent of my towel. I checked my side and saw that a bruise was forming where the board had hit me. It was sore, but it was going to be okay. We drove out to Madaket, the westernmost part of the island, and ate fish tacos at a place called Millie's, where Ben knew the bartenders.

Later, we sat on the beach and watched an orange sun drop into the sea. I'd never seen a sky so red. It was as if the sun had left a memory of flames that was brighter than actual flames. The lowest sky glowed like coals. Above it, hot pink clouds skidded into a purple night. As the sky darkened, the ocean carried the colors in ripples and shocks.

I thought of those salmon-colored pants called Nantucket Reds. They were a copy of a copy of a copy of the most tepid version of this sky, the real Nantucket Red. I thought of Zack, acting like nothing had happened between us, treating me as if I were any old girl, despite the fact that we had been in love. *In love.* And it just seemed so lame to me, lame like those stupid fucking pants.

Ben put an arm around me, resting his hand on my hip. He was here. His arm had weight and warmth. He was real.

His heart was alive enough to have been broken. He leaned into me. "Can I kiss you?"

"Yes."

He pulled me close, tilted my head back, and pressed his lips to mine.

We kissed on the beach until a dad approached us, several toddlers in tow, and told us this was a "family setting." We burst out laughing. He grabbed my hand as we walked to the car and we barely let go on the drive back to Fair Street. Then we kissed in the Land Rover in front of the inn as we shared the most basic details of our lives, the kind of stuff I'd known about Zack forever. Ben told me he was twenty-two. *Kiss.* He grew up in Maine. *Kiss.* He graduated from Sarah Lawrence College last year. *Kiss.* He was helping Sadie fix up her house. *Kiss.* He'd lived in Brooklyn until May, when he came to Nantucket. *Kiss.* He didn't think he was going back.

"Because of . . . what's her name?"

"Amelia." He disappeared for a second.

"What about you?" He touched my neck. "Where are you from?"

"Providence."

"Go on." His hand traced my collarbone.

"I'm eighteen."

"Thank god." His finger dropped to my breastbone, outside the T-shirt.

"Nineteen soon. I'm going to Brown."

"We've been over that." We both laughed.

He ran his hand through my hair, tugging on it a little

as he went for another kiss, and I had the feeling that guys his age either kissed or had sex but didn't do anything in between. But before I even had a chance to tell him to slow it down, he surprised me by transitioning into a hug, telling me he had to go check on Sadie, and planting a chaste kiss on my burning forehead.

Liz was drinking wine out of a jam jar, making her way through a sleeve of Oreos, and watching *Big Brother*.

"Holy hair extensions," I said, as the girl on the TV twirled her mane and addressed the camera. I sat next to Liz on the sofa.

"Yeah, but Shayla's really cool," Liz said. "She's going to win this whole thing. What's going on? Did you do it with Mr. Bartender?"

"No. I'm just getting to know him."

"Watch out. He's probably a right ass." Liz refilled her jam jar with wine and reached for another cookie. "They all are. Men are not to be trusted."

I didn't have the heart to remind her that she was the one who had told me I didn't need to be such a very, very good girl. And I wasn't going to ask her if "right asses" spend their summers fixing up their grandmothers' houses.

"You're probably right," I said. I snuggled under the covers with her and laid my head on her shoulder. She passed me the Oreos and I took one. "Liz, are you okay? I heard you crying last night."

She paused the TV. "I keep going over it in my head,

trying to locate the moment."

"What moment?"

"The moment I lost him. But I can't find it. Where did I go wrong?"

"You didn't do anything wrong," I said, as fat tears rolled down her pink cheeks. "He lied. He's a right ass, remember?"

"But why doesn't he want to be with me?" she asked, hiccuping. "What's wrong with me?"

"Nothing's wrong with you." I handed her a tissue. She blew her nose loudly.

"I sound like a stupid, stupid girl. I sound like a bloody Phil Collins song."

"You aren't stupid. Shane's stupid. You're badass!"

"Do I look badass?" she asked, gesturing to her oversize Cranberry Inn T-shirt and pajama bottoms with kittens on them.

"You look . . . casual. Hey, remember when you bought me that thong last year? And made me unwrap it in front of Gavin?" She laughed, snorting a bit. "Or how everyone on this island, including the rich and famous—*especially* the rich and famous—know and love you? Or the fact that you stayed out on Nantucket instead of doing what everyone expected?

"I suppose that was adventurous."

"It was badass! You're only twenty years old and you're running an inn."

"A stupid person might have more trouble, it's true."

"See? Exactly." I turned back to the TV and grabbed an Oreo. "Now, tell me why Shayla's going to win."

Twenty-two

THE WAMP'S LOBBY DELIVERED THE CLASSIC NEW ENGLAND elegance that its shingled exterior promised: wooden floors, white wicker furniture, a fireplace, vases of blue-purple hydrangeas, lush potted plants, and a coffee setup that with silver spoons, sugar cubes, and china cups, was at least 30 percent fancier than the one we had at the Cranberry Inn.

"I'm a guest of the Claytons," I said to the front desk girl.

"Cricket, right?" When I heard her husky, party-girl voice, I realized she was Thonged Snoring Girl. "Jules is waiting for you on the beach." From the way she was looking at me, it was clear she was trying to place me. I couldn't wait to tell Liz.

"I'm a waitress at Breezes," I said. "It's my day off."

"No wonder you look so familiar." She lowered her voice. "Weren't you gonna move into the Surfside house with us?"

"I found something else."

"That's too bad. It's like a constant party. We didn't go to bed until like five this morning."

"Sounds fun," I said.

"So, if you want to change into your suit, the Claytons' cabana is number sixteen." She pointed down a hallway. "Just go all the way to the end and make a right. It's the last one."

The cabana was actually a simple wooden changing room built right over the sand. The door to number sixteen was open. Inside were some little closetlike rooms for changing, a shower, and several hooks for bathing suits and towels. I knew that if Nina were alive she would've loved to decorate this little space. She would've hung the perfect photo or an antique mirror above the white dresser.

I could see how each of the family members had claimed some small corner for their own. Here was Jules's nook, with her boyfriend jeans, shampoo, and razor lined up on a bench. There was Mr. Clayton's corner, with his large flipflops, sunglasses, and a vat of sunblock, SPF 75. There were Zack's things, hanging on hooks: his blue bathing suit, still wet; the towel with the Tropicana logo that he'd used all last summer; his Whale's Tale T-shirt, inside out.

I had been hoping Ben's kiss would cure me of Zack. But I grabbed Zack's shirt, brought it to my face, and inhaled until I was light-headed and flooded with memories of last summer. *Sunscreen, sand, salt water, him.* I flipped it over and smelled the back, coaxing every last bit of Zackness from its fibers.

Ben's kiss was expert, just like his hands. He knew when to move in, when to pull away. He knew when to press and when to release. And it worked: my body responded without waiting for my thoughts. It had been different with Zack. We belonged to each other when we had kissed. I buried my face in the shirt one last time before reminding myself that he didn't belong to me anymore. I was about to hang the shirt up on its hook when I decided to stuff it in the bottom of my beach bag instead. I folded my clothes and placed them over it and made my way down the pathway to the beach.

When I stepped onto the hot sand, one of the Wamp employees sprang to his feet and offered me a cup of ice water and a towel. I didn't know if I was supposed to tip him. Since I was wearing only my bathing suit it was pretty obvious that I didn't have any cash on me.

"It's okay," he said. "Are you looking for Jules?"

"Yeah." Who was this clairvoyant beach boy?

He laughed. "She told me you were coming. She's right there."

He pointed and I saw Nina wearing one of her signature black bikinis, her hair in a messy bun and her sunglasses on her forehead. She was reclining in a beach chair under a yellow umbrella, reading a magazine. I couldn't wait to tell her about Rodin at Cisco. I couldn't wait to make her laugh.

"Why are you looking at me like that?" Jules asked, startling me out of my mistake. I adjusted the beach chair next to hers. "Do I have kale in my teeth? I just had a salad."

"No," I said. "It's nothing."

"Whatever you say. Since when did everyone decide kale tasted good, anyway?" She handed me a magazine. It was *Vogue Paris*. "For you. It's not like I can read it, but you probably can."

"Cool," I said, and opened it up, testing out my French.

"Parker brought it from Paris."

I dropped the magazine on the sand, not even bothering to close it. I was about to ask Jules what she was trying to do in bringing up Parker, but then I noticed the page the magazine had opened to. It was a piece about Rodin. I couldn't believe it.

"My mom loved this guy." Jules picked up the magazine and dusted off the sand. Her eyes narrowed as she studied the glossy spread.

"I know." I propped myself up on my elbow and debated telling her about the list. I'd already come up with a plan for the second item: *Learn to drive and then drive Route 1 to Big Sur*. Nina didn't know how to drive, because she had grown up in Manhattan. I knew how to drive, but I didn't know how to drive stick. I was going to ask Ben to teach me in the Land Rover.

Jules pressed her hands against the page, flattening it for the best view. "She doesn't like art."

"Who?"

"Jennifer. I'm not sure what she's into besides my dad."

"He's probably just having a fling."

"He'd better be." She flipped the page and inhaled a perfume sample. "Do you hate Polly?"

"No," I said, thinking. "It's just, she's not my family, and my dad wants me to pretend like she is, and I have to do it all the time."

"That sucks," Jules said, flipping through the pages. "But she is family, right?"

"She's *his* family," I said.

"But he's *your* dad."

"I don't want to think about it." I stared out at the water. "Let's go for a swim."

She got up and I followed her, but turned back when I realized I was still wearing my sunglasses. I could see the Breezes staff setting up for dinner. I could see Amy looking out at me from the porch, a hand on her hip, her bright red lipstick visible from here. I wondered if Ben had told her that we'd hooked up. I wondered if I was her Parker. I was not going to be anyone's Parker. "Hey," I called. I smiled and waved.

"Is that girl giving you the finger?" Jules asked.

"Yup," I said, continuing to wave. "She sure is."

Twenty-three

"NO, NO," BEN SAID, AS THE LAND ROVER STALLED YET again. "You need to lift your foot off the clutch while you put your foot on the gas."

"I did."

"You have to do it *at the same time*. Like I've been telling you. For an hour."

"That's what I was doing," I said, tapping the steering wheel with my palms.

It was the first time I'd seen Ben tense. Even on Saturday nights when the bar was slammed, he moved as if knowing that the world was going to wait for his easy smile, sun-lightened hair, and faded shirts. Now, on these sandy back roads, a little furrow disturbed his smooth brow.

"I was lifting my foot gently off the clutch just like you said," I insisted. He pointed at my foot, which was still depressing the clutch. I jerked it away. "I mean that's what I *did*. Seriously, when it was happening, that's what I was doing. I swear."

He tilted his head and raised his eyebrows as if he didn't believe me. I sighed, trying desperately to appear even-tempered and in control. I was going to drive this Land Rover if it killed me.

"Here's the thing. If you don't lift your foot off the clutch, the gear can't catch," Ben said, sounding like someone's dad. "Want me to draw you a picture?" I glared at him. "Whoa. Okay. You want to take a break?" He put a hand on my knee. "Sadie is expecting us for dinner soon."

"No," I said, pushing his hand away. "I can get this."

His cell phone rang. He paled as he glanced at the number and silenced it. Was it Amelia?

"I'm ready when you are," he said.

I took a deep breath and turned the key. It wouldn't start. "Shit."

"You're foot isn't on the—"

"I know!" I took another breath and pulled an old lacrosse trick: visualizing. In lacrosse, it was the ball landing in the net I saw in my mind's eye. Now, it was the car traveling effortlessly down the road. I started the car again, releasing the clutch as I applied my foot to the gas—*at the same time*—and we started to move.

"Yay!" I said. "Yay, yay, yay!"

"All right, nice job." He rubbed his hands together. "Now we're cooking with gas."

"Oh, shit, oh, shit, oh, shit," I said as I saw another car approaching. These back roads had been ours alone for an hour now. Why did other people have to show up now? "There's another car on the road."

"That'll happen from time to time, but you got it," he said, tilting the steering wheel toward him to give the other car, which was full of kids headed to the beach, enough room to pass.

"Good work. Now you're going to shift into second gear. This is easy, since you're already moving."

"Okay." I pressed on the clutch and shifted. Ben whistled.

"I like second gear," I said, unable to suppress a huge smile. "Second gear is, like, my favorite."

"You want to drive all the way to Sadie's?"

"I'll try," I said, exhilarated by my triumph. He directed me down a few roads and casually turned on the radio. Fleetwood Mac was singing "Gypsy" on the classic rock station from the Cape. Mom loved this song. I knew every word. I was so focused on the task at hand, so deep in my concentration, that I started to sing along quietly without even realizing it.

"You have a pretty voice," Ben said. "I didn't know you could sing."

"Thanks, but I can't. My mom's the singer."

"You sound good to me," he said, tossing off one of his gorgeous smiles.

"I don't have perfect pitch," I said. Mom had checked my pitch a few times and even though she tried to hide it, I knew it disappointed her that I hadn't inherited her gift. Somewhere along the line, I'd decided that if I couldn't sing perfectly, I wouldn't do it at all.

"It's not about perfect," Ben said as the road changed from dirt to paved. "It's about expression."

Two trucks peeled out from a big driveway and trailed us. Ahead, a stop sign loomed. My grip on the wheel tightened.

"Oh, god," I said, eying my rearview mirror. One was a gigantic Suburban and the other a Ford Expedition.

"One foot on the clutch, one foot on the brake," Ben said as we approached the stop sign.

I did what he said, and miraculously, the Land Rover came to a halt.

"I did it! I did it!" We high-fived. Once the road was clear, I stepped on the gas, forgetting all the little steps I was supposed to do between. Something screeched. I tried to get us going again, choosing two different pedals. The car lurched.

"My transmission!" Ben said. My back was sweating. My thighs were sticking to the seat. I couldn't remember which pedal was which and I didn't want to touch any of them. Behind me, the driver of the Ford Expedition leaned on his horn.

"What the hell?" the driver called out the window.

"Calm down, dude," Ben said under his breath.

"Can we switch?" I asked Ben as the guy pressed on his horn again, this time sticking his middle finger out his window. He kept jabbing it higher and higher. "Uh, we have to switch."

"Okay. Turn the car off."

I did and we both climbed out of the car. But then the car started to roll onto whatever main road I'd been trying to turn onto. It was moving on its own! An oncoming car slammed on its brakes, forcing the car behind it to do the same.

"Jesus," Ben said, as we ran alongside the car, opened the doors, and climbed inside. It wasn't rolling fast, but it was the first time I'd ever jumped inside a moving car. Ben did whatever it was people who drive stick know to do, and we pulled over to the side of the road. The Expedition guy shouted something as he turned in the opposite direction.

"I, um, forgot the emergency brake," I said.

"I know," he said. And we burst into laughter as he started the car. I was laughing so hard that I almost didn't notice that it was Parker's car that had slammed on the brakes and was now passing us. Her dark hair streamed out the window like a raven taking flight. Zack was in the passenger seat, craning his neck to get a better look at me. I knew in my gut that he'd seen the whole thing. The Rolling Stones came on the radio. I turned up the volume, put my feet on the dash, and sang my heart out.

Twenty-four

"AND THESE WERE MY PARENTS, HARRIET AND BERNARD, Broadway actors. They were part of the 'Sconset Actors Colony back in the Roaring Twenties," Sadie said, pointing to a photo of a dramatic woman with a draped Grecian dress and a wreath of flowers in her hair, striking a pose next to a man who was lounging on a porch looking both guilty and delighted with himself. "My parents built this cottage themselves."

"That's this cottage?" I asked, taking a closer look at the picture. "Where we are right now?" Ben sat next to me with a fresh beer, and I tried not to squeal as he slipped a cold hand between my lower back and the sofa. Sadie's house was tiny, with one bedroom, one bathroom, a little kitchen, and a living room that doubled as Ben's bedroom at night. We were both couch surfing this summer.

Sadie was older than I'd thought. From the way Ben had spoken about her, swimming in the ocean every day and peppering her speech with her favorite four-letter words, I'd imagined her to be the same age as Polly's parents, Rosemary and Jim, and neither of them had gray hair. But Sadie was old-lady old, with white hair and watery eyes, even though she'd lit up like a teenager when she'd seen Ben waving to her as we headed into the driveway.

"You don't recognize it because so much has been built up around it," she said. "You used to be able to see the ocean from the porch."

"And there was an actors' colony on Nantucket?"

"There certainly was. And what free spirits they were," she said, turning the page to reveal a sepia-toned group hanging out on a porch. Some were smoking pipes, some were wearing crazy hats. Some were in costumes and others in bathing suits, but they all looked like they were having the time of their lives. "They came out here to write and act and make music and, let's face it, get laid."

"I warned you about her," Ben said, smiling, sipping his beer, and sliding that hand farther down my back.

"I had no idea. I'd always thought of Nantucket as a vacation spot, not a place where artists go."

"Nantucket has always been a place for oddballs and wanderers; that's the nature of an island." She turned another page, to a picture in which a busty girl in a bikini posed in the sand. "Oh, that's me, the summer I met Ben's grandfather. We made love for the very first time on that beach."

"Wow," was all I could think of to say.

"We had fun in the old days," Sadie continued. "Now I don't know what young people want."

"We want the same stuff," Ben said.

"But these kids driving seventy-thousand-dollar cars? It's like they're already middle-aged. I didn't want fancy cars when I was young. I wanted adventure. Sex. Romance. The open road."

"Cricket almost got us killed on the open road today," Ben said, and I pinched his leg.

"But it takes money to travel and be free," I said, thinking of Parker and her new Parisian wardrobe, Jules's graduation car, Nina on the Amalfi Coast.

"No, it doesn't. During these summers, I didn't have a dime," Sadie said. "No one did. Didn't bother us. Look." She pointed to a picture of a bunch of people standing around a fire on the beach. Some were drinking beer. Some were laughing. Some peered pensively at the fire. A handsome guy with one of those rockabilly hairstyles was playing the guitar. She tapped the face of a girl who was dancing. "That's me, in a dress I made from Mother's curtains. Fun is free, as they say, and adventure is there for those who look for it. Especially on a warm July night in Nantucket." She placed a cool, soft hand on my cheek.

Sadie loved Nantucket as much as Nina did, but in such a different way. Nina had worn designer clothes and wanted to join the most exclusive club. Sadie was a waitress, dancing on the beach in a dress made of curtains.

"Okay, kiddos, I'm going to turn in. Up she goes," Sadie said, hoisting herself off the sofa. "I didn't have my nap today, and I'm tired. Benjamin, take Amelia to the beach and show her the stars. Somehow, on Nantucket, the stars are closer."

"This isn't Amelia," Ben said. His voice lowered. "She's gone, remember?"

"Sorry." Sadie shook her head. "Of course. Force of habit."

Did I look like Amelia? Had she come here with Ben? How many times? I wanted to ask Ben, but his mood had downshifted. His eyes had darkened and were far away.

"There's a comet that's supposed to be visible soon," I said, grasping for the lightness that had been present just moments ago.

"Larsen's Comet. It's visible now," Sadie said. "Great idea! Go have a look."

"I think she's kicking us out," Ben said as Sadie headed into her room with a glass of water and a book under her arm.

"Can we go to that beach and build a bonfire?" I asked, pointing to the picture of Sadie and her friends.

"We're not supposed to," Ben said, sounding like himself again. "But we can."

Ben led me down a path through a grove of trees to a fire pit in the sand. The breeze off the water was chilly. I sat down in the sand and pulled my Brown sweatshirt over my knees. I stared up to see if I could spot the comet, but it was cloudy. I could only see the moon and a couple of very bright stars.

Ben unloaded some wood and newspaper from a canvas bag and built a mini-tepee with wood. As he lit the newspaper, he explained that fires weren't allowed on the beach without a permit, but that it was almost impossible to see the bonfire from the road.

"What would happen if we got caught?" The flame caught the paper and jumped to life. Ben's face was focused and glowing in the firelight. There was something about watching him build a fire that was making me aware of my breath, my heartbeat, and the way they worked together.

"We might get arrested."

"What?"

"Yeah, they're cracking down," he said, enjoying my discomfort. "And it all goes in the newspaper."

"Really?"

"Karla does not like to see her staff in the *Inky*." Ben stood up, admired his work, and dusted off his hands. Normally, information like this would have made me want to snuff out the fire and head back home, but I fought the impulse. Ben said no one could see us from the road. And besides, he had picked up his guitar, and the fire was dancing. The air was swirling with cool, salty breezes and heat from the flames, and the surf was whispering, *Stay, shh, stay, shh, stay, shh, stay.*

I realized Ben was strumming "Gypsy." He started to sing and I joined in, thinking that the words reminded me of Nina. But no. They didn't. They reminded me of Sadie. No. They reminded me of my own mom, singing in the kitchen and in the car. They reminded me of myself, dancing around the living room when I was a little kid. I was remembering a part of me that I'd forgotten about, or maybe I was seeing a glimmer of the person I might become. A girl who was free. A girl on the open road. A girl singing on the beach. I felt connected to something. Something in the moon and the fire and the ocean. I felt a light stream of electricity in my limbs. A sense of belonging to this moment, this place on earth—an ancient kind of happiness.

"What are you thinking about?" Ben asked. "Scoring lacrosse goals at Brown?"

"No. Not at all."

"When do you start practice?"

"I don't know." The idea of lacrosse startled me out of my open-road reverie. I hid my face in my palms, feeling guilty. Lacrosse. I'd put off practice for weeks now. I dug my heels into the sand and inhaled the beach air. The dagger of panic was sharper than ever. It was pointed right at my throat.

"What?" Ben asked.

"Nothing," I said, burying my head in my arms. The future was vast and open, so why was I headed back to Providence, to do exactly what I'd done all through high school, in the same small city I'd lived my whole life?

"What is it?" he asked.

I couldn't bring myself to say it aloud. I shut my eyes as that feeling of connection, of inexplicable security and feather-light joy, vanished like a wisp of smoke into the night.

Twenty-five

LATER, I COULDN'T SLEEP. AS I WATCHED THE SKY LIGHTEN from black to purple, I debated as to whether I was making a big mistake by staying in Rhode Island for college. I pulled the sheet over my eyes and wondered if I even cared about lacrosse anymore. It was not like I'd even read the last two e-mails from Coach Stacy. I hadn't gone running in over a week. *What did that mean?* I asked myself as I breathed under my cotton tent.

At three thirty I got out of bed, pulled out my acceptance letter to Brown, and turned on the kitchen light. I smoothed out the letter on the kitchen table, reread it, and remembered what it had felt like to get in. How Mom had screamed as the mailman called, "Congrats!" over his shoulder. How I'd slipped the letter to my dad at Jake's Diner, telling him very casually that I had something interesting for him to read. He hooted, then popped a quarter in the jukebox and jitterbugged me around the restaurant. I remembered the new looks of respect I received from everyone I told. Mrs. Hart, the ancient English teacher, kissed me on the forehead. Jim and Rosemary were offering me eight thousand dollars so that I could have the full Ivy League experience. I remembered the speech Dad gave in my mom's driveway at my graduation party, saying that he "couldn't be prouder."

How could going to Brown University, *the* Brown University, ever be a mistake? That was impossible any way you looked at it. And of course, I cared about lacrosse. Of course, I loved it. I poured myself a glass of cold water and drank it all. I closed my eyes and remembered the rush of scoring a goal, the smell of warm grass on a spring afternoon, the pasta dinners with the team the night before a big game. I laid my head on the cool, indifferent kitchen table and repeated the words *I'm doing the right thing. I'm doing the right thing. I'm doing the right thing.* I crawled back to my bed, the sofa, and fell asleep as the first birds were starting to sing.

"He's going to propose!" Jules said as she flew through the door of the inn's laundry room.

I was so in my own world, so exhausted, nursing a coffee as I folded yet another load of the inn's signature cranberry-colored towels, and Jules was so out of context that it took a minute to register her as real and not a figment of my imagination. My arrangement of covering for Liz two mornings a week was great for my bank account, because I wasn't paying rent, and I was still very grateful to her, but it was almost impossible for me to catch up on rest.

"Cricket, hello; did you hear me?" Jules asked, her fingers rigid and fully extended. She was dressed for work at the Needle and Thread in a white miniskirt, Tory Burch flats, and a scarf tied artfully around the handle of her purse. Her hair was blown out in perfect waves. But there was chaos in the details of her face: the wrinkled forehead, the frantic eyes, lip gloss that went just beyond the boundary of her lower lip.

"I'm sorry. Propose what?" I was so tired, so taken by surprise, that her words didn't quite make sense.

"Marriage!" She huffed at my slowness.

"Who's getting married?" Was she talking about Zack and Parker? Would that even be legal? My heart rate dragged, despite three cups of coffee. I leaned on the hot, rumbling dryer.

"Dad!" Jules said, the cords of her lean, pale throat tightening like strained wires. "Who else?"

"To that girl? Are you sure?"

"Yes. My dad is going to propose to Jennifer, a woman he met three months ago on Friendly Adults dot-com."

"Oh, no," I said. *Friendly Adults dot-com?* I wasn't sure, but I thought that was a kinky Web site. Like, XXX. "You think, but how do you know?"

"I saw the ring." She started to pace as much as the small laundry room would allow. "I was looking for this picture of

Mom in her vintage von Furstenberg dress; you know, the one where she's actually talking to Diane von Furstenberg at a party?"

"Yes," I said. I knew the picture. Nina was wearing one of her signature wrap dresses and a dramatic necklace, holding a martini. I remembered looking at that photo and thinking, *This is what I want to look like when I grow up.*

"I wanted to show it to Maggie, my boss. And for as long as I can remember, Dad kept it in a drawer by their bed. So I went looking for it. But I didn't find it. Instead, I found a ring." Jules began breathing rapidly, fanning herself. For a second I wondered if she was going to faint. I pushed a little stepladder toward her. "A big, fat, cheesy engagement ring."

"Hold the phone," I said, using one of my mom's phrases as Jules lowered herself onto the stepladder. "You don't know he's going to propose to her. That ring could've been your mom's."

"It wasn't my mom's. It was a new ring. It was tacky as fuck. I know it's for her. It was just the kind of thing she thinks is beautiful. Mom would never wear it." She shook her head and looked at her watch. "And now I'm going to be late for work." She placed a trembling hand at her temple, grabbed one of the freshly folded Cranberry Inn towels, and held it to her face, shoulders shaking.

"It's okay," I said, rubbing her back as she let out a sob and blew her nose into the towel. "Go ahead. Make yourself at home." We both laughed.

"I have to go," she sighed.

"Call me later, okay? We'll figure it out," I said, although I wasn't sure how. These were adult problems. I'd learned from my parents what could be controlled and what couldn't. If Jules was right, this was one of those things that couldn't, and she was just starting to get a taste of how much it was going to suck.

"Okay," she said, holding her breath in an attempt to stop crying. She was looking at me as if I might actually be able to make this all right.

"So I've started the list," Liz said as she walked in, a notebook under her arm. I had promised Liz that when she woke up we would make a list going over the pros and cons of her moving back to England or staying in America. She, too, was dressed for work, but hadn't quite managed to pull herself together. What with the circles under my eyes, Jules's runny nose, and Liz's ill-buttoned shirt, we were a sad crew. "Oh, hello," Liz said to Jules. "We can have fresh towels delivered to you. What room are you in?"

"I'm not staying here," Jules said, dabbing her eyes with the towel.

"How did you know where to find me?" I asked Jules.

"I just looked around. I opened doors until you were standing behind one." I laughed. It was so Jules, so blazingly confident.

"Pardon, but who are you, exactly?" Liz asked.

"Jules."

"I've heard about you," Liz said and crossed her arms.

"Good things, I hope?"

Liz shook her head no.

"We had a rough time last year," I said and shrugged.

"Yeah," Jules said, as if last summer had been a very, very long time ago. "We did."

"Hey," I said. "What did Zack have to say about all this?"

"I didn't tell him." She watched sudsy sheets going around in the washer and said quietly, "I only wanted to talk to you. Hey, you know what I want, like, more than anything? One of our adventures."

In the old days, our adventures involved sneaking into dances at the boarding schools within driving distance and playing "exchange student," or putting balloons under our shirts and walking around the mall like regretful pregnant teens, or taking the bus to Boston and getting hot chocolates at the Four Seasons Hotel. During those excursions we created our own world. We moved in sync, spoke in code, and laughed so hard that hot chocolate came out of our noses.

An adventure with Jules would be the perfect escape. Between waitressing and covering for Liz, I hadn't had a single day off since I'd landed on Nantucket. I had almost four thousand dollars, but I was tired. Tired of taking drink orders and carrying plates of calamari and never being able to catch up on sleep. And last year, Liz had been my wild yet sensible British ally, buying me lingerie and texting me sex tips. But ever since her breakup, she was in bed by eight thirty. She'd stopped wearing mascara. Her walk had lost its swagger. I'd seen my mom go through heartbreak.

I'd watched her retreat into a mental castle and pull up the drawbridge, and something similar was happening to Liz. Once again, I was on the other side of the moat, unable to reach the lonely lady. Yes, an adventure was in order.

"I have the best idea," I said. Our eyes met in mischief.

"Yay!" Jules gave me a quick, hard hug. "Text me."

Watching her leave, I felt like I'd just heard an old favorite song on the radio.

Liz squinted in concern. "Be careful, insect."

Twenty-six

"NASTY!" I SAID AS I SPIT THE CAMPARI OUT IN THE Claytons' kitchen sink and guzzled water directly from the tap to wash away the bitter, medicinal taste. Jules was laughing her really laughing laugh. The one that was mixed with snorts and gasps, and that I hadn't heard in almost a year.

"Why did you get this stuff?" Jules asked, wiping a tear away.

"It looks so pretty," I said, admiring the ruby liquor with the stylish, European label. I couldn't tell her that it was because it was number three on Nina's life list: *Drink Campari on the Amalfi Coast with Alison.* Even after her laundry room breakdown, even though I'd felt comfortable enough to spit in her sink, I was still scared she'd tell me that Nina was her mom and I had no right—*no right at all!*—to follow that list, copy it, inhabit it, make it mine.

"You're not supposed to drink it straight. It's one of those things you mix."

"Why didn't you tell me as I was pouring myself a whole glass?" I asked, holding up the juice glass I'd filled three-quarters full without even an ice cube. "I mean, it looks like fruit punch."

"I wanted to see what happened," she said, and laughed again. "Besides, you never drink. I wasn't about to stop you. You missed that night at the secret bowling alley. And tonight is all about fun!"

We'd been texting for a few days, trying to plan our adventure. Since Liz seemed to have secret connections everywhere, I had asked her to get me a bottle of Campari. And then tonight, when it was slow enough to send one of the waitresses home early, I'd volunteered and texted Jules immediately.

Me: Are you up for some Campari and a midnight dip?

Jules: Hells yeah! Come over. Dad in NYC.

Mr. Clayton had said he was on a business trip. Although Jules's theory that he was going to propose hadn't been confirmed, it seemed pretty likely that it was true and was going to go down soon, maybe even this weekend. Jennifer was with him and the ring was missing.

I headed to the fridge to find a mixer for the Campari. Jules turned on her iPod and played an old Katy Perry song we used to dance around to. I noticed a picture of Zack and Parker on the fridge. Their arms were around each other and they were in front of some ivy-covered building at their boarding school. He's probably with her right now, I thought. I flipped it over and stuck the magnet back on it. I opened the fridge, grabbed a can of Sprite, and drank it down. The Campari flavor mixed with the sweet soda.

"Sprite and Campari is a different story," I said. Jules was dancing around the kitchen. I poured the Sprite into a glass, added Campari, and took a long swallow. "Yum."

"Make me one," Jules said. I poured her a taste.

"Nice," she said, taking a sip and considering. "Tart and fizzy. I know. I'll fill up thermoses. We'll take our drinks with us."

"Sassy and classy!"

"Goofy and glamorous!" She hit *repeat* on the Katy Perry song.

"Bitter and sweet, like love!" I added dramatically, and I spun out of the kitchen, right into Zack. Our eyes met and locked.

"You're not supposed to be here," Jules said to Zack. "Did you have a fight with Parker?"

"None of your business," Zack said.

"Whatever. We're leaving." Jules grabbed a monogrammed canvas bag that she'd had as long as I'd known her and put the thermoses in it.

"Where are you headed?" Zack asked.

"None of your business," Jules said, mimicking his tone.

"We're going on an adventure," I said. "We're going to Steps." I wanted him to know that if he could traipse all over our magical island, well, so could I.

"Oh, yeah?" Zack said, leaning against the door frame. "What are you going to do there?"

"We're going for a swim," I said, raising my eyebrows, a hand on my hip. Teaming up with Jules had given me a dose of my old confidence. "A midnight dip."

"Towels! Can't forget the towels." Jules took off for the laundry room.

"Hey, have you seen my Whale's Tale shirt?" he called after her.

"No!"

"Steps, huh?" He asked me. The night we'd gone skinny-dipping there was the moment I knew I was in love with him. It had been a perfect night. Bright moon. Summer air. Dark water. When we moved, the water glowed with phosphorescence.

"Yes. Steps," I said, watching a slow smile spread over his face.

"I saw you the other day. Like maybe a week ago. Out on Milestone Road. You were, like, jumping into a Jeep with some guy?"

"Ben." I nodded. Tucked my hair behind my ear. "He's teaching me how to drive stick."

"Ha! I bet he is," Jules called from the other room. "Woo-hoo!"

"That guy works at Breezes, right? At the bar?"

I nodded again. Zack crossed his arms and shook his head. "I've seen that dude around." He lowered his voice to a whisper. "You're not falling for that shit, are you?"

"You just don't know him," I said, throwing what he'd said to me about Parker back at him. "You haven't given him a chance."

Jules returned, the canvas bag now stuffed with towels, and tripped over the threshold. "Whoops!"

"Are you sure this is a good idea?" Zack asked. "You guys seem kind of drunk."

"I'm not drunk," I said, though I could feel the Campari warming my joints. Tipsy, I thought, as Jules linked an arm in mine and I leaned on her; I'm tipsy.

"Besides, it's late," Zack said.

"We'll sleep when we're dead," Jules said, and we marched out the door, soldiers of silliness.

"So, what's going on with this Ben guy?" Jules asked as we kicked off our shoes and descended the stairs to the beach. "Is he your boyfriend?"

"Yeah," I said, though I wondered if I would I have answered the question like that if he had been standing next to me. "Are you and Jay going to stay together next year?"

"Absolutely," she said. "That's why we're going to school in Boston." As soon as we hit the sand, we stripped to our suits, took sips from our thermoses for courage, and made a run for it into the water. We screamed with delight as we dove under the surface. We shut our eyes against the salt and kicked up into handstands and floated on our backs.

"I could just forget everything out here," Jules said, breaking the silence. "Maybe when we're both in college next year we can come here for a weekend. Like when it's snowing."

"We'll go for a polar bear swim," I said, and dove back under, sliding through the water like a fish. I grinned at the thought of being grown-up enough to have a weekend away with just my friend. I grinned because we were talking about our future as friends, and I knew that we had surmounted the hurt that had fallen like a massive tree between us last summer. I grinned because I felt free for the first time since I had arrived on the ferry. Held by the Nantucket Sound, I unhooked myself from my worries. Water filled my ears, closing out the world. Lacrosse didn't exist here. Brown was far away. I felt cleansed. *Sadie was right,* I thought, and came up for a breath, *fun is free.*

"I'm getting cold," Jules said when I resurfaced.

"Okay. Let's head in." My bottom lip was trembling, too. Also, I was starved. I hadn't eaten since the staff meal at four. I noticed we were farther from the shore than I'd realized. "Whoa. We drifted."

"Yeah, let's go," Jules said, her face serious. We were both good swimmers, and made silent and effortful progress to the beach. I could feel myself working against the tide, and the Campari, and was relieved when we finally reached the shallow water.

"Holy shit," Jules said, "There's a man on the beach and he's looking right at us. Cricket, we're going to die!"

"That's no man," I said, laughing. "It's Zack."

"What are you doing here?" Jules called to Zack as we climbed out of the water, teeth chattering.

"Every summer there's a story about someone who drowns," he said, and handed us each a towel. "I didn't want it to be you guys."

"Thanks," I said, shivering and wrapping the towel around me. For a minute, I saw the old Zack: unguarded and kind.

Jules looked at him sideways as she roughly dried off her legs. "Since when did you get so concerned with my safety?"

"I've always been concerned with your safety," he said.

"Turn around. I'm going to change," Jules said. "Don't want a yeast infection."

"Why do you have to be so nasty?" Zack said, turning around and shielding his eyes with his hands like we were going to play hide-and-seek.

"Well, Zack, it's what happens to girls when they walk around in wet bathing suits. And we all know you're no stranger to fungus," she said. She turned around, ripped off her bathing suit, and put on her underwear and bra. I wrapped the towel under my arms, tucking it in on itself so it wouldn't fall off, and slid my wet bathing suit off under it.

"You're never going to let me forget about that, are you?" Zack asked.

"Nope," Jules said, laughing as she hopped into her jeans.

"You know, that was over a year ago, and the doctor said it was perfectly—" he said, turning around. "Normal." We made eye contact. Jules was facing away. I watched his gaze travel from my discarded bathing suit to my bare shoulders. When our eyes met again, his were soft, pleading. A blue flame burned in my chest, but I signaled for him to turn around. He did. I let my towel fall, stepped into my shorts, and grabbed my T-shirt.

"There's something else you should know," Jules said, pulling her shirt over her head, "since we're on the subject of ugly truths and you've decided to care. Dad is proposing to Jennifer."

I froze. I really had been the only one she'd told. Zack turned around.

"What? Are you serious?"

"I found an engagement ring," Jules said. "It wasn't Mom's."

Twenty-seven

THE THREE OF US WALKED BACK TOWARD TOWN ON CLIFF
Road. It was empty and quiet. The houses were still with
sleep, and the darkness was weightless and unthreatening.
The cool air held the smells of the daytime: beach roses,
sandy towels, and sun-warmed pavement. I couldn't hear the
ocean, but I could sense it, close by, lulling the island. It was
the nighttime of dreaming children. The only sounds were
our footsteps as we walked in the middle of the street. Jules
and I drank from our thermoses. Zack took swigs from a
bottle of vodka that Jules had brought as backup.

"I thought he was just 'getting back out there,'" Zack
said.

"Me, too," Jules said.

"She's too young," Zack said.

"She's too stupid," Jules said.

"She has cats," Zack said.

"She's never been out of the country," Jules said.

"She's Republican," Zack said.

"She's not even funny," Jules said.

"She doesn't even like us," Zack said.

"What will happen to Mom's stuff?" Jules asked.

"Will she want to have kids?" Zack asked.

"It hasn't happened yet," I said, stopping this runaway train of thought. "He might not do it. Your dad is a good man. A smart man. He married your mom."

Over the next stretch of road, we walked again in silence. Jules walked ahead. She had gallantly offered to carry our wet towels and suits, and the damp canvas bag bumped against her hip. Zack hung back near me. A car sped by, and he changed places with me so that he was walking closer to the road. Our pinkie fingers brushed and my pulse jumped. Two steps later, our shoulders touched. My cheeks burned so that the air felt cold. His palm crossed mine, and the shock of it nearly transformed me into an electrical impulse, one that could travel on telephone wires. When Zack held my hand, I gasped with pleasure.

I brought the thermos to my mouth and drank until I was dizzy with Campari and confusion as Zack and I ran our thumbs over each other's knuckles. We swayed as we walked. I knew I needed to let go of him, and that he couldn't just show up and hold my hand after the distance he'd put between us, but instead I held his hand tighter. I told myself I would allow myself ten more seconds of touching him. I counted slowly, savoring each second. *One one thousand, two one thousand, three one thousand. . . .* I was at seven when Jules called, "Do you guys smell that?" Zack and I dropped our hands.

The delicious smell was coming from Something Natural sandwich shop. The ghost of homemade bread hovered in the air and beckoned us into its driveway. My mouth was actually watering.

"Wait, they're not open. What're we doing?" I asked as we walked closer, realizing that my words weren't coming out right. I couldn't quite catch up to my thoughts. "Uh, I think I'm drunk." I giggled, plucked a hydrangea blossom from a bush, and tucked it behind my ear.

"Yes," Jules said, laughing as we locked arms and tripped closer to the building. "You are!"

"I need a picture of this," Zack said, turning on his camera phone, but not before dropping it on the ground; he picked it up and fumbled with the buttons. He was even drunker than I was. "I need a video."

"Why?" I asked, leaning toward him.

"So when we're old we can remember we were kids once," he said.

I tilted my head back and breathed in the night. "Look at the sky," I said, arms extended, walking in an uneven circle. I just knew at that moment that Nina was with us. She was watching us and wanting us to be together. Jules and me as best friends. Zack and me as a couple. Together, our own kind of family.

"This is us," Zack said, holding the camera away so that it was facing us, and we were in the frame together. He put an arm around me, and I tilted my head so that it was resting on his shoulder. He turned to face me. Our lips brushed in an almost-kiss. Then he tilted the camera to the sky. "And this is the middle of the night." He turned the camera back on us. "This is us in the middle of the night."

"Give me the camera," Jules said. Zack handed it to her. "And put your arms around each other." We did. "You guys look so happy it's not even funny." She handed the camera back to Zack. "And I'm so hungry! I'm so hungry I could faint!" She sat on the ground.

"Poor Jules," I said to the camera. "She's so hungry."

"And drunk," she said. "I'm very, very drunk."

"Me, too!" I said. "I, Cricket Thompson, am so very drunk."

"You know what I need?" Jules said.

"What do you need?" I answered. "I'll get you anything you need!"

"I need a sandwich!" she said, rolling onto her stomach. "I need a sandwich like I've never needed anything before in my whole life. Turkey and avocado. Oh, and cheddar. On Portuguese bread."

"Then a sandwich you shall have!" I said.

"But they're not open," Jules said, waving a finger. "I checked."

"But there's an open window," I said. "If I stand on your back, I bet I could climb inside."

"Look what happens to the angel with some Campari in her," Zack said, staggering behind me with the camera.

"I've got the devil in me, too," I said.

"Oh, yeah, Miss Brown Lacrosse Player?" Zack asked.

"Don't remind me about lacrosse. I haven't practiced lacrosse in, like, weeks," I said. "Now, do you want a sandwich, too? Give me your order. I'm an expert!"

"Roast beef!" Zack proclaimed. "With mustard and lettuce and tomato."

"That sounds good. We want roast-beef sandwiches," Jules said, stumbling to a standing position and then squatting by the open window. "Climb aboard, birthday girl."

"Sandwich party!" I said.

"Don't forget the Portuguese bread!"

Was I really going to do this? To climb on Jules's back, through an open window, and make sandwiches? Yes, I was. I'd missed out on my senior-year fun. This was one of the best things about Nantucket. It can make you feel so separate, so out to sea. Untouchable. For the first time ever, I felt like one of the people who belonged here. That was how the Claytons had made me feel before Nina died, that I had a place in the world. It was right next to them.

We were all laughing as I hoisted my body through the

window. "I'm in!" I called as I landed on a countertop. I lowered myself into the kitchen sink. I tried to orient myself as my feet found the floor. I knocked into a dishwasher and felt around until I located a light switch and turned it on. Digging out my tip money from my pocket, I pulled two twenty-dollar bills and put them on the counter. That would more than cover the cost of three sandwiches. I smiled, imagining the staff wondering about where that money had come from. Then I took a few extra bucks and stuck them in the tip jar, because we food-service workers needed to help each other out. There was a knock on the door, and I made my way out of the back room and into the front, expecting to see Zack and Jules waiting for me.

"Coming!" I called. I saw an apron hanging up with the Something Natural insignia on it and thought it would be a nice touch to answer the door with it on. Then I saw a box of latex gloves and giggled to myself, thinking how this would really complete the outfit. But when I opened the door, it wasn't Jules and Zack standing on the other side. It was the cops.

Twenty-eight

"OH," I SAID TO THE TWO YOUNG, GOOD-LOOKING OFFICERS. "I was just going to make a sandwich." They looked like people I'd grown up with, just a little older, like someone's big brother and maybe a cousin from New Hampshire. So in the first few seconds after I opened the door, I wasn't that nervous, just surprised. They knew I was a good person, the kind of person who obeyed the rules 99.9 percent of the time, right? Everyone knew that.

I mean, I knew I wasn't *supposed* to be inside of Something Natural, but it didn't feel like I was doing something wrong, either. I had left forty dollars on the counter and a tip in the jar, even though I was my own server. In fact, there was something that felt right about being in Something Natural in the middle of the night. I loved this place. I knew my way around a kitchen. I was planning on cleaning up afterward.

And all that Campari didn't feel like a bad thing, either. It had given me energy and off-kilter bravery. It had pushed glitter through my bloodstream, and, like a liquid magnet, it had brought Jules and Zack and me together again. For the past few hours, the world was a party to which I'd finally been invited.

But the stern eyes and straight mouths of the officers clarified the situation. I took in their heavy shoes and their big, bright flashlights and my good feeling went away. So I tried to explain again, but my tongue felt slow and sticky. I couldn't get my words to come out right no matter how hard I concentrated.

When the blond officer asked me to step outside and began to read me my rights, while the other went into Something Natural to "check for damages," I was so surprised, so scared, so turned upside down that I vomited right into one of the hydrangea bushes from which just a half hour earlier I had plucked a blossom.

Jules and I were arrested and taken to the police station, where we were fingerprinted and had our pictures taken. We were both charged with underage drinking, but I was also charged with the more serious offense of breaking and entering. It was a misdemeanor, the officer said. *A misdemeanor.* I didn't know what the word meant, but it scared me past the point of crying. I was going to throw up again.

The officer must've seen my color change, because he asked if I needed the bathroom. I nodded, clamping my hands over my mouth, certain now I was going to vomit. He let Jules accompany me while I ran down the hallway, barged into a stall, and hung my head over the toilet as the Campari rose again in a burning, acidic wave. Afterward, I sat on the closed toilet seat, shaking. Jules dampened a paper towel and held it to my head.

"It's going to be okay," she said.

"What happened to Zack?" I asked, wiping away a tear.

Jules whispered that she'd given Zack the thermoses and the bottle of vodka and told him to run. She didn't want to get charged with possession of alcohol or open-container violations. He was drunker than both of us combined. "There was no need for the three of us to go down. He's either at home or passed out in the bushes somewhere." She pressed the paper towel to my clammy forehead.

When we returned from the bathroom, the bail commissioner was there, and because I had my tips in my pocket, I was able to pay our bail amounts, which were forty dollars each. He told us that we needed to appear in court a week later and we signed forms promising that we would.

"If I were you," the bail commissioner said, a meaty finger pointed right at my heart, "I'd get a lawyer."

"Why didn't you run away when Zack did?" I asked later that night in Jules's bedroom. It was my first time in her Nantucket bedroom, which was a lot smaller than her Providence one, with one single bed, a small desk, and one window. There was evidence of Nina in the rug, the mosaic of family Polaroids arranged like a quilt, and the high-quality sheets. Neither Jules nor I wanted to sleep alone, so she lent me a T-shirt and pajama bottoms and we arranged ourselves head to toe in her single, iron-framed bed. We still didn't know where Zack was, but at least he hadn't been arrested.

"I couldn't leave you alone," she said as she handed me one of the pillows from behind her head. "I got you drunk."

"You didn't exactly force it down my throat. You didn't make me drink." I thought of the heat and excitement of Zack's hand passing over mine, how it had almost been too much happiness, how I'd swallowed the Campari in gulps.

"This is going to sound kind of crazy," Jules said, lying back and staring at the ceiling. Her feet, in socks with little Santa Clauses on them, were next to my face.

"What?"

"I could feel Mom there." She was whispering, even though we were the only two people in the house. "It was like I just knew she wanted me to . . ."

"What?" I felt her breathing next to me.

"Stay with you." She exhaled. Silence enclosed us like a canopy of trees. We stepped into its cool, leafy darkness.

After a few minutes I said, "You know that picture you gave me? Of your mom when she graduated from Brown?"

"Yeah?"

"On the back it has a list, a life list, of things she wanted to do."

"It does?"

"I think she must've written it right after she graduated.

She lists five things. And one of them is about drinking Campari with Alison in Italy."

"So that's why you brought Campari," Jules said, lifting herself onto her elbows.

"Yes."

"What else is on this list?" Jules asked, sitting up and drawing her knees into her chest. She looked like she was about seven years old as she tilted her head and bit her lower lip. I knew it had been wrong to keep the list from her.

"Let's see," I said, sitting up. "Well, the first one is *Visit the Rodin Museum in Paris.*"

"She definitely did that, like, ten times. What else?"

"The second one is *Learn to drive and then drive Route 1 to Big Sur.*"

"She did that when she was pregnant with me."

"And then there's *Drink Campari on the Amalfi Coast with Alison.*"

"What else?" Jules asked.

"She wanted to be in a Woody Allen movie," I said.

"I wonder if she ever was."

"It's checked off," I said and shrugged. "So she must've been."

"Wait a second." Jules drummed on the coverlet. "She told me about this. I'd forgotten. She was cast as an extra, but she wasn't in the movie."

"Which movie was it?"

Jules covered her mouth with both hands. "Oh, Cricket, you don't want to know."

"I do." I kicked her under the covers. "I really, really do."

"I'm sorry, I can't tell you. Not right now." She was trying not to laugh.

"Jules, what was it?" I asked, grabbing her feet, holding her toes hostage.

"It was—" Jules began, but she couldn't finish, because she was laughing too hard, snorting and crying, the works.

"What?" I asked, as serious as she was ridiculous.

"It was . . . *Crimes and Misdemeanors*."

"No," I said, shaking my head. "This can't be what she meant."

"Cricket!" Jules was laughing so hard she was wheezing. "We got arrested."

"They put us in the patrol car and we got fingerprinted," I said, and I started laughing, too.

"We had mug shots taken," she said. "We're outlaws."

"We've committed crimes and misdemeanors," I said. We were crying and laughing and laughing and crying.

"I'm crimes and you're misdemeanors," Jules said as we clutched our stomachs. We fell off the bed we were laughing so hard. We rolled around on the rug, tears streaming down our faces. We crawled to the bathroom so we wouldn't wet our pants. We were releasing the tension of the day, of the night, of the whole year. We laughed until we were so exhausted that we were communicating exclusively in grunts and giggles and sighs, until we finally fell asleep, her Santa Claus feet in my face. I never did get to tell her about the last thing on Nina's list.

Twenty-nine

I WASN'T LAUGHING WHEN I WOKE UP AFTER ONLY A FEW hours of sleep. For a moment, I thought maybe it had all been a dream, or a nightmare, but when I realized I was wearing Jules's Rosewood Basketball T-shirt, when I felt my head pounding and saw the ink on my fingertip, I knew it had actually happened. I had been arrested for breaking and entering and underage drinking. Jules was still asleep. I tiptoed through the rest of the house, looking for Zack. When I opened the door to what had to be his room, he wasn't there. I checked my phone to see if I had any texts from him. There was the one he'd sent last night. The picture of the two of us. The moment came back to me. I typed out a text: I love us in the middle of the night. My finger hovered over the send button for a moment before I hit it, and listened to it whoosh away from me.

"What happened to you?" Liz asked when I showed up back at the inn. She made us a pot of coffee and I told her the story. I told her everything, the details coming back to me in startling, crisp detail as I recounted the night: the skinny-dipping, climbing through the window, vomiting on the hydrangeas.

"Jules is horrible!"

"It wasn't her fault," I said. "I got drunk all on my own. It was my idea to make the sandwiches." When I described the officers, she knew exactly whom I was talking about. She said that the blond one in particular was on a personal mission to crack down on the summer kids. All traces of Liz's depression seemed to vanish as she went into crisis mode. She made me an omelet and wrote a list of what I needed to do. It was Liz's idea to call Paul Morgan, the lawyer who was my mom's friend. I still had his card in my wallet.

"It's very early for a social call," he said when he answered my call at eight a.m.

"It's an emergency," I said.

"A legal one?"

"Yes," I said, choking back tears. "Yes."

"Come over in an hour."

It was also Liz's idea that I write a letter of apology to the owners of Something Natural. She knew them from spending the winter on Nantucket and would personally deliver the letter to them. "Stuart and Jill are reasonable people," she said. "And they'll appreciate a note." She also said that I needed to talk to Karla as soon as possible. If I could get to her before my name showed up in the police blotter, I might have a chance of keeping my job.

"My job," I said, shutting my eyes and shaking my head, realizing that if I got fired, I'd lose my opportunity to live in the dorms next year. I was several thousand dollars short of my goal. Jim had been very clear that I needed to have all eight thousand for him to match my earnings. I felt a sharp, shooting pain in my side. I'd have to explain to Jim and Rosemary what had happened. I'd have to explain to everyone. I started crying all over again.

Liz led me from the inn's kitchen to the manager's apartment. She started a hot shower for me and laid out a fluffy clean towel, my best skirt, and a blouse that she herself had ironed within a starched inch of its life. She blew out my hair and applied a tasteful amount of makeup. She helped me compose a letter to the owners of Something Natural, and by that I mean she dictated it to me.

"I sincerely regret having crawled through the window of my most favorite sandwich shop, thereby violating not only you, but also the sacred trust that exists among neighbors on Nantucket," she began. I was incapable of forming my own sentences, so I copied her words, hoping that her charming British inflection would somehow seep into the ink. When I'd finished the letter and she'd checked it for mistakes, we delivered it to their mailbox.

We drove to Paul Morgan's house on Orange Street. I was shaking as we approached his door. "I'm so scared," I said.

"Come on now," Liz said. She rapped with the shell-shaped knocker with confidence and placed an arm around my waist. "Just stand up straight and tell him exactly what happened."

Paul answered the door, looking freshly showered and grave. He led me into his living room and gestured to the sofa. Liz sat next to me and took my hand as I explained what happened. Paul took notes on a yellow legal pad. I sweated through my blouse in several places.

"I screwed up," I said, my voice shaking. "But I swear I didn't mean it. I paid for the sandwiches. I even left a tip in the jar. Not that that excuses anything, but . . ." I dissolved into tears.

"Calm down," he said. "Take a breath and walk me through the whole thing." He crossed his long legs and listened as I told the story.

"Breaking and entering is no joke," he said, when I finished the sordid tale. "And neither is underage drinking."

"I know," I said, wiping my tears. "It was the first time in my life that I've been drunk. I'm so ashamed."

"Take it easy. I'll defend you," he said. "When do we go in front of the judge?'

"Tomorrow," I sobbed. "I have almost four thousand dollars. Will that be enough for your fees?"

"Honey, I'm not going to charge you. And hey, do you

have any idea how many kids this happens to every summer?" He handed me an actual cloth handkerchief.

"How many?" I asked. "Tell me."

"Many," he said. "I'm not saying that what you did wasn't
very serious. I'm not saying that it's in any way excusable.
But we're going to do the best we can. There have been
presidents of the United States who've done far worse than
climb through the window of a sandwich shop."

"Thank you," I said, throwing my arms around him.
"Thank you so much."

"Okay, kiddo. Take a deep breath."

"Are you going to tell my mother?" I asked, ending the
one-sided hug and taking a short, sharp breath.

"I'm *your* lawyer," Paul said, pushing his Prada glasses up
his straight, patrician nose. "This is between us."

I don't know that I'd ever loved anyone more than I did
Paul at that moment.

"Karla? I've had an incident," I said thirty minutes later
after Liz had marched me over to Breezes, insisting that
I get this over with as soon as possible. Liz waited for me
outside in the car. Karla was sitting at her desk, filling out
purchase orders. I sat down in the cold, metal folding chair
opposite her.

"What kind of incident?" she asked

"The kind you're going to read about in the police blotter," I said.

She dropped her pen and sighed. "Oh, Thompson." She shook her head. "Oh, boy. What happened?"

I recounted the story for the third time that day. The repetition was giving me a chance to find the narrative and tell it faster. I focused only on the salient details: a girl who'd never been drunk before does something really, really stupid and gets caught.

For the first time, I avoided tears, but Karla was not charmed. "What kind of an idiot breaks into Something Natural?"

I proceeded to beg and plead as I had never done before. I told her I was sorry. I told her I'd never even been drunk before and I didn't intend to be again anytime soon. I told her I'd written a letter of apology to the owners of Something Natural.

She rubbed her eyes. "I have to think about this."

I told her all that was at stake for me. I told her about Rosemary and Jim. I told her about having to live at home if I couldn't earn the money I'd promised. I told her how good I'd been at saving everything I'd earned. I pulled a crumpled bank deposit receipt from inside my wallet, smoothed it out, and passed it to her.

"I don't need to see that," she said.

"I'm different from the other summer kids. I work hard."

"We're all hard workers," she said, flicking the receipt back at me. "That doesn't make you special. It only means you meet the minimum qualification for the job."

I nodded, shoving the bank receipt in my pocket and my humiliation down deep. I stared intently at the wood grain of her desk, darkened by a new shade of shame. "I'll clean the cappuccino machine every night until . . . it shines like the top of the Chrysler Building." It wasn't until after I said that that I realized I was quoting *Annie*.

Karla sighed from some very tired place. "I said I'd think about it."

"When will you let me know?" I asked, licking my dehydrated lips.

"When I'm ready," she said, waving toward the door and giving me a look that said *get out of here*.

"I'll be ready when you are," I said with as much confidence as I could muster.

"How'd it go?" Liz asked when I walked back outside. It was a mercilessly beautiful summer day. The sky was royal blue. The birds sounded like they'd flown straight out of an animated movie and into my nightmare. "Did she fire you?"

"No," I said as I shut the car door and secured my seat belt. "But she didn't *not* fire me, either."

I glanced at my phone. Still no word from Zack. I texted him again: R U ok? Then I texted Jules: Is Zack ok?

"What are you going to do?" Liz asked. "What's the plan?"

"Show up anyway."

Thirty

I ARRIVED EARLY, IN A CLEAN SHIRT, PRESSED KHAKIS, AND full makeup to try to hide my hangover, which had not gone away by three o'clock as Liz had promised it would.

"Rough night?" Ben asked, as I went behind the bar to grab a Coke.

"You have no idea." Had I cheated on him last night when Zack and I held hands and almost kissed? I wasn't sure. Were Ben and I even going out?

"That's some serious concealer you've got going on." He tugged on my T-shirt. "You want to tell me about it in the fridge?"

"No!"

"Whoa." Ben lifted his hand and stepped back three paces.

"I'm sorry. It's just . . ." I stepped toward him and whispered, "I'm not even supposed to be here. I was arrested."

"What?" He furrowed his brow in concern. He leaned on the bar, listening, as I told him the short version. "I didn't know you had it in you."

"What's that supposed to mean?"

"Nothing bad. What were you drinking?"

"Campari and Sprite."

"Campari and Sprite? *Sprite?* Have I taught you nothing?" He reached for my hand.

"I can't." I sidestepped him without a smile as I saw Karla emerge from the kitchen.

Karla paused when she saw me, but seemed to accept my presence. The restaurant filled up fast, and she didn't send me home. It was the busiest night of the summer, and she wouldn't have made it through the shift short a waitress. I was a machine, working strong right up until closing, even on only a few hours of sleep. I was shaking with hunger and fatigue at the end of the shift. I was stained with coffee and wine and sweating through my T-shirt, but I stayed late and cleaned the cappuccino beast until it gleamed. Then I counted my tips and put them in the jar Karla kept on the bar for her charity, Operation Smile, all two hundred fifty dollars. It was a penance. I put my arms on the bar, laid my head down, and had a small moment of reprieve.

I didn't know Karla was watching until she gave my shoulder a rough squeeze and said, "Hope you have a backup shirt for tomorrow night's shift. The one you've got on is a mess."

"Thank you," I called as she walked back to the office, wiping tears of pure exhaustion from my cheeks. "Thank you so much."

It was then that I noticed a text from Jules. He's fine. He spent the night in Lily Park. Showed up around 11 today.

So he just wasn't going to text me back? After all that we had been through? After me getting arrested? I would've thrown my phone across the room, except I couldn't afford a new one.

The court date arrived quickly. Paul defended me, explained that this was a first-time offense, that I had a stellar academic record and numerous character references, and that it was the first time I'd ever been drunk in my life. He emphasized the fact that no windows had been broken and that I hadn't actually made any sandwiches. The police confirmed that not only had nothing gone missing or been broken, but also that I'd left forty dollars on the counter and a tip in the tip jar. I guessed that this and my letter had made an impression on the owners of Something Natural, because they decided not to press charges. I was required to stay out of trouble for six months and to write a composition about the dangers of alcohol abuse.

The judge dismissed both Jules's case and mine. I thanked Paul. I leapt into his arms and planted a lip-glossed kiss on his smooth, moisturized cheek. Jules and I walked out of the courtroom arm and arm, a pair of free women. Instead of the whole, heavy world, it was only the midday sun that rested on our shoulders.

Jules, Liz, and I went out for a celebratory lunch at the Brotherhood of Thieves. Liz felt this was the only appropriate place for a burger and fries. Whatever problems she had with Jules she had decided to put aside for the moment. Jules was in the middle of telling us the story of Zack's night spent sleeping in Lily Park and later being awakened by a group exploring Nanucket's natural flora when I interrupted.

"I texted him," I said. "Twice. He never texted me back."

"He's in deep shit right now," Jules said, shaking her head.

"We're the ones who got arrested," I reminded her.

"I saw what was going on between you two that night, by the way," Jules said.

"What do you mean?" I asked. She didn't look mad about it. She was smiling.

"Oh, come on, the hand-holding, the whispering, the kissing."

"The kissing?" Liz asked.

"We didn't kiss," I said. Jules cocked an eyebrow. "We brushed lips."

They burst out laughing. Jules slurped her Coke. Liz slapped the table.

I blushed. "What?"

"Brushed lips," Liz repeated and wiped her eyes. "That's

rich! Listen, I have a big surprise for your birthday. You must make sure you get the evening off."

"Oh, yeah! My birthday is next week. I'm going to be nineteen." After such a stressful few days, it was a relief to think of something as normal as a birthday.

"In a year you'll be 'in your twenties,'" Jules added with an ominous air as she squeezed one stripe of mustard and one stripe of ketchup down the length of one of my french fries.

"Don't act like we're that different. You're only three months younger than I am."

"Shut up, the pair of you," Liz said. "I'm twenty." She lowered her voice and nodded toward the bartender. "But don't tell Jack over there. He thinks I'm twenty-two."

"I can't believe you've already planned something for me, Liz," I said and rested my head on her shoulder.

"Course!" Liz said. "That's what friends do."

"Obviously I have your morning planned," Jules said, stealing another one of my fries. She'd ordered a salad instead of fries with her burger, but she clearly had no intention of touching it. "Because of our usual ritual. The one we've done for years now." Every year since we'd known each other, Jules and I had had waffles on our birthdays and brought out the stuffed pig, Lulu, whom we had co-adopted from FAO Schwarz on my one and only trip to New York with Jules and Nina in the eighth grade. Last year, Jules had tried to carry out the ritual, but she'd walked in on Zack in my bed. I was worried our birthday ritual had been ruined forever, so I felt a happy relief that she'd mentioned it. "But what do you want to do after that?" she asked.

"I think, after this whole mess, I just want to go the beach and have fun," I said with a sigh. "Good, clean, summer fun."

"Perfect. You two can come to the club!" Jules said. I noticed with surprise that she was including Liz, who had left her out of the evening invitation.

"You know I love those cabana boys in their polo shirts, but I have a business to run," Liz said. Her phone vibrated. "That's the inn phone now." Jules rolled her eyes, but luckily Liz didn't notice; she was back to her efficient, inn-running self, even if she did still get teary-eyed at the Samsung commercial with the guy who looked like Shane in it. She finished replying to a text and looked up. "My only request is that you're back at the inn by five for the surprise."

"I can do that, and I'd love to come to the beach club, Jules," I said. "Can I bring Ben?"

"Hells yeah. I wouldn't mind seeing him in his bathing suit," Jules said. She raised her Coke. "To good, clean, summer fun."

"I prefer a bit of dirt with my fun, but okay," Liz added, lifting her wineglass.

"To escaping the long arm of the law," I said, joining with my lemonade. And we all drank to that.

Thirty-one

ON MY BIRTHDAY, I WOKE UP EARLY TO THE CHIMING OF the bells from the gold-domed tower of the nearby church. Liz brought me, on a tray with a pitcher of cream, a piping hot cup of coffee, which I sipped on the hammock in the garden. The morning was balmy and sweet with the scent of freshly mowed grass and blooming gardens. The air hummed an August tune. Mom called to tell me the story of the day I was born. Dad called a few minutes later and sang "Happy Birthday" into the phone and promised a back-to-school shopping trip when I came home.

When each of them asked me how the summer was going, I felt a pinch of guilt replying, "Fine." I didn't tell either of them about getting arrested or about my day in court. It's not like they read the *Inquirer and Mirror*, and

Paul Morgan had sworn secrecy, so they were unlikely ever to find out. Everything had ended up just fine, so why not wait to tell them until I was much older and we could laugh about the whole thing? Right now it would only have needlessly worried and disappointed them.

Jules picked me up in her graduation Jeep with Lulu the stuffed pig in the backseat. We drove to the island airport, where Jules had promised they served the best breakfast on the island. We both ordered waffles, of course, and big bowls of cappuccino with extra foam, and guessed about the lives of the travelers coming and going with their rolling luggage and Vera Bradley bags. Jules covered Lulu's ears when she asked for a side of bacon. When our cappuccinos arrived, I luxuriated in the knowledge that I wouldn't have to clean the machine that produced them.

On our way back into town, my phone dinged with a text. It was Ben, wishing me a friendly "happy birthday!" and I texted back a friendly "thanks!" I was happy to hear from Ben, but at the same time, it reminded me that I hadn't heard from Zack and probably wouldn't. He hadn't texted me after I'd been arrested, so why would he contact me on my birthday?

"Hey, cheer up," Jules said as she parked in front of Needle and Thread, the fancy Main Street boutique where she worked. "We're going to go shopping. I'm going to let you use my employee discount."

"But I thought you'd get fired if you let your friends use your discount," I said.

"The boss is in New York," Jules said. "I'll just say I bought it for myself."

As soon as we stepped into the store, Jules started chatting up her coworker, Jennie. I spied a red bikini.

"What do you think?" I asked when I stepped out of the dressing room.

"Hot," Jules said.

"Red hot," Jennie echoed.

"It's actually kind of conservative," I said, turning around in front of the three-way mirror, noting its full coverage of boobs and butt and the innocent bows at the hips.

"But that's what makes it hot," Jules said. "It leaves something to the imagination. It's asking the world, *Good girl or bad girl?*" She stood behind me, took out my ponytail, and shook my hair over my shoulders.

"Girls can be both," I said.

"Of course. We women are very complex."

"Guys are, too," I said, thinking of Zack, so sweet one day and so harsh the next.

"Yes, humankind is full of contradictions. We could write a thesis, but I'd rather go to the beach," Jules said. "So I'm buying you this red bikini."

"Jules, are you sure?" I asked.

But she had already clipped the tags and was whispering with Jennie at the cash register.

"You girls want to sit next to Zack and Parker, right?" the cabana boy asked when Jules and I made our way down the boardwalk, she in Nina's black bathing suit and I in my brand-new red bikini. He picked up two blue recliners and nodded to the left. "They're right there."

I shook my head.

"Actually, I think we'll sit over there," Jules said, pointing to the opposite end of the beach. "As far away as possible."

"You invited Parker?" I asked Jules. The sand was soft and deep and still morning-cool as we walked down the beach, the cabana boy trailing a few feet behind us with our chairs. "On my birthday?"

"She belongs here," Jules said under her breath. "I can't tell her not to come here. Her family practically owns this place. Even on your birthday."

"Oh." She had a point. I looked over my shoulder. Parker was stretched on a recliner in an aquamarine cover-up that looked expensive even from here; one leg dangled as she read a magazine. Zack was sitting next to her in the sand on his Tropicana towel, reading a book. What was he reading? What was he thinking? Did he remember it was my birthday? Did he know we were coming?

Jules thanked the cabana boy as he set up our chairs, then turned to me. "Besides, what do you care that she's here? You look amazing." She flapped her hand at me. "Text your bartender. Tell him to join us."

"Okay." I sent Ben a text. I looked back up at Jules and felt a wave of affection. She was back. My best friend was really back. Ben replied immediately. "He'll be here in an hour," I said.

As usual, Jules and I couldn't sit still for long. After about ten minutes of sunbathing, we started tossing the Frisbee. When that became boring, we challenged ourselves to take a step back with every successful connection. Then we had to incorporate a funny dance into either the catch or the release. We switched it up to see how deep we could go in the water and still complete the pass. This was one of the things I loved best about Jules. She was always in motion. Wearing Nina's black bikini, she looked like her mother, but only in repose. She moved like her own girl.

I caught Zack staring in our direction a few times, but every time I returned his glances, he looked away. Ben arrived. "Look at you!" he said when he saw me in my new suit. He joined in our Frisbee game, and Zack started openly staring. And then, when we were playing Monkey in the Middle and Ben tackled me, Zack actually came over. Parker followed, arms crossed as her aquamarine cover-up billowed out behind her in the breeze.

"Are you guys going to play?" Jules asked.

"I am," Zack said, taking off his T-shirt. His body. So familiar. Mine, I thought.

"I'm just going to watch," Parker said in her husky, party-girl voice. Now that she was in front of me, I noticed she didn't look so good. Her Grecian-style cover-up made her elegant from a distance, but up close, something was off. There was a hollowness in her eyes, a sallowness to her skin. It looked like she needed protein, a cheeseburger, maybe. Or at least some blush. But who needed blush on a perfect summer day?

"So what are we playing?" Zack asked.

"Frisbee football," Jules said. "You see where that sea-weed is? That's one end zone. And the other one is over here." She jogged down the beach away from kids, babies, and fancy people under umbrellas, and drew a line in the sand by dragging her heel, placing a piece of driftwood at one end and a bunch of seaweed at the other. "It's me and Zack versus Cricket and Ben."

"This is like Ultimate," Ben said.

"Basically," Jules said, "but tackling is allowed."

"Hee-haw!" Ben said.

"We're on the same team," I reminded him.

"Oh, yeah," Ben said.

"Are we going to let the birthday girl win?" Zack asked. So he did remember.

"No way," I said. "Play your heart out."

"So you can pivot but not run with the disk," Jules said. "If it gets intercepted or you don't complete the pass, it goes to the other team. The first team to get three points wins. Cricket, since it is your birthday, you get the first pass. Zack, if you let me down, your ass is grass."

"Shut up, Jules," Zack said, and tossed the disk to me, fast, hard, and direct, and I caught it with one hand.

"Damn," Ben muttered under his breath. "Girl can catch."

"Girl can also throw," I said with a smile as we back-tracked to our end zone. "Go long." I released the disk in a perfect, sailing arc. Ben leapt into the air and caught it. Jules tried to guard him, but Ben was agile, and with one sharp pivot, he tossed it back to me. Zack was all over me, but wasn't taking advantage of the tackle rule.

"Go, Zack," Parker called from the sidelines.

I saw Ben was in the zone, so I tried a skip shot, and sure enough, it briefly touched the ground and bounced. Ben caught it, raised it over his head, and whopped.

"One–zip," I called.

Jules and Zack conferenced before they mounted their counterattack.

"Come on Zacky," Parker called as she clapped.

My stomach flipped. Zacky. Bleccch!

Jules and Zack advanced toward us in a series of short passes, but I intercepted one and tossed it to Ben, who pivoted and tossed it back to me, and we scored again. It was almost too easy.

"It's not looking good, guys," I said, a little breathless as I passed the disk to Jules.

"But you are," Ben said, bumping hips with me. Zack looked like he was going to be sick.

"Time out," Jules said. "Zack, get your ass over here." That was the other thing I loved about Jules. She was seriously competitive. Ben and I drifted toward the water for our own little huddle.

"You're good," Ben said, and took a quick dunk. As he stood up again, the water slid down his body.

"I've been trying to tell you," I said, wading into the water with him.

"Tell me what?" he asked, pulling me toward him for a kiss.

"I'm a lot better at sports than I am at waitressing." We kissed, lightly, tastefully.

"Let's do this," Zack said, clapping his hands.

"I want to play now," Parker said, stepping out of her gossamer cover-up. Her horse-jumping legs didn't seem as rock-strong as usual. She was thinner than I remembered.

"We can't have three against two," Jules said.

"We can handle it," Ben said.

"Yeah, bring it on," I said.

"Okay, then," Jules called. "You cocky bastards."

"The literary term is *hubris*," Zack added.

"Call it whatever you want. We just say 'kicking ass,'" Ben said.

Zack whispered something to Jules and she nodded. Then she flung the disk way out into the Nantucket Sound. I could barely see it.

"What the hell?" Parker asked as Zack started swimming for it, a little leisurely, I thought.

"What are you waiting for?" Jules asked me. "That bikini is made to move."

I dove into the sound and swam hard. Zack was now doing the backstroke, so it wasn't hard to gain on him. Besides, the current was pushing the disk in my direction. I was actually going to beat him to it if he didn't pick up the pace. He was practically treading water.

"Cricket," he said, as we grabbed the disk at the same time. I was completely out of breath. "Put your feet down. We're at the sandbar."

I touched the soft sand with my feet. I knew my face was bright red with exertion. I coughed up some water and gave myself a chance to catch my breath. I was about to jerk that disk from his hand and turn back to shore when he yanked it from my hand instead. He pushed it underwater and stood on it.

"What are you doing?"

"I wanted to talk to you. Alone." He looked back at the shore, where Parker, Jules, and Ben were watching us.

"How are you?" he asked quietly.

"I'm okay," I said in disbelief. "I mean, besides the fact that I was arrested and had to go to court."

"You must've been so scared," Zack said, touching my arm underwater.

"What are you doing out there?" Parker called from the shore.

"We're looking for it!" Zack called back.

"I'll help you," Parker said.

"I was so scared," I searched his green eyes. "I texted you."

"I know," he said, taking my hand. Parker was swimming toward us, fast. "I couldn't text you back, but I wanted to tell you how much that night meant to me. I know we were drunk and you got arrested, but other than that, I loved it."

"Other than that," I said, laughing. His eyes softened. *He'd said "love."*

"Happy birthday, Cricket," he said, squeezing my hand. "I'm trying to be a good person right now. I'm trying to do the right thing. You have to trust me."

"What are you talking about?" I asked.

"Do you love that guy?" he asked.

"I don't know. Do you love her?" I hated that we were tossing *that word* around like the Frisbee he was currently standing on. We'd only used *that word* when we truly meant it.

"I'm protecting her," he said. "I owe it to her."

"But you don't owe anything to me?"

Parker popped up. "What's taking you guys so long?"

Zack and I held each other's gaze for another breath. There would be no high five, part three. Ever. I dove under, freed the disk, and held it up high. "Found it," I said, loud enough so they could all hear me.

"Frisbees don't sink," Parker was saying as I started back. The salt water disguised my tears as I swam back to where I could throw it to Ben. I was ready to win this game and get out of here.

Thirty-two

AFTER OUR 3–0 FRISBEE FOOTBALL VICTORY, AFTER I'D
thanked Jules with a big hug and politely said good-bye to
Zack and Parker in the name of sportsmanship, Ben and I
left the club holding hands. He said he wanted to take me
somewhere. He had to be back at Sadie's in time to change
and get to work, but when he glanced at his watch, he said,
"That gives us plenty of time." I was in my wet bathing
suit, a towel around my waist, when Ben told me to take
the driver's seat. I followed his directions out of town to a
remote part of the island, down a quiet road. Ben told me
that we only had access because Sadie had a special permit
as a trustee of the Wildlife Refuge. I drove the whole way,
only stalling once. Ben took over when it came to driving on

the actual beach. There was hardly anyone out here except for a few fishermen thigh-deep in the gentle, foaming surf.

We parked near a dune, and Ben pulled out a blanket and a cooler from the back of the Land Rover. Then he took my hand and led me over the hill of sand to the perfect hiding spot. We were surrounded by dunes on all sides. He smiled up at me as he spread the blanket out, and I realized he'd brought me there to have sex.

So far, we'd had all of these external obstacles that made sex logistically difficult. I wasn't about to take him back to the apartment with heartbroken Liz, and he wasn't going to invite me to spend the night on his grandmother's sofa. We couldn't even exchange longing glances at work without risking our jobs. The Land Rover had been our make-out mobile, but even that had its limitations. The seats didn't recline, and the backseat was boxy and too short in both directions. But that had been okay with me. I liked how if we tried to recline all the way, we'd bump our heads or jam our knees. I liked the obstacles.

But here, in this warm white valley of sand, with the sun burning above us and the lulling waves so close, there were no obstacles, unless you counted the eelgrass, the wild beach roses fretting in the breeze, or the solitary cloud that lay haphazardly at the bottom of the sky. As I joined him on the cool cotton blanket and he gallantly removed my TOMS one by one, I felt myself shaking. I needed to tell him up front how I was feeling.

"I'm not ready to have sex," I blurted out.

"That's okay," he said. "That's not why I brought you here."

"Oh, come on," I said, joke hitting him. "The blanket?"

He laughed a little. "Can't blame a guy for trying, can you?" He pulled a flask from the little cooler.

"What's that?" I asked.

"A Bicyclette. Every girl should have a drink. And a Bicyclette is yours, I think. It's refreshing, spunky, and a little surprising. It's Italian white wine and your favorite, Campari."

"Don't say the C-word!" I said, my mouth cottoning at the thought. He threw back his head in a laugh, and I noticed the place where the top of his chest met the hollow of his throat. I wondered what it would be like to have sex with him. I had only ever had sex with Zack. I had only loved Zack.

Maybe I still did love him, I thought, remembering what it had been like to hold his hand the night we'd gotten in trouble, and how as soon as our fingers interlaced the world had clicked into place. I thought of what it had been like to be face to face with him on the sandbar earlier, how I could've sworn I still saw love in his green, LASIKed eyes. But no. I remembered what it had felt like when he didn't text me back after the scariest moment of my life. That had felt like a punch. Love wasn't supposed to feel like that.

"Are you sure I can't tempt you?" Ben asked and uncapped the frosty metal container. "The Campari and wine work together to create a new flavor, and it whets your appetite. Come on, it's *your* drink."

"I'm on probation."

"One sip," he said, inching closer.

"I guess if it's my drink, I should at least try it. One sip." I brought the cold flask to my lips and drank. Ben was right. It was refreshing, bright, almost startling, but it also had that familiar Campari aftertaste and my stomach clenched.

"Too soon?" he asked.

"How can something so pretty be so bitter?"

"I brought iced tea, too," he said, and handed me a Nantucket Nectars.

"Yum," I said, guzzling the sweet drink. He took a long swallow from his drink. Then he touched the cold flask to my shoulder. "You're burning up. Take this." He unbuttoned his white shirt, took it off, and handed it to me.

"Now you'll burn."

"No, I won't." Ben was one of those people with skin that caramelized in the sun.

I put on his shirt. It was soft and worn.

"So what's the story with that kid?" Ben asked, leaning on an elbow.

"What kid?"

"You know who," he said, smiling, one hand spidering my kneecap.

"Oh. Zack. We used to . . ."—I paused, held my breath, and considered—"go out."

"I could tell," Ben said, but he didn't sound jealous. He tilted his head, his eyes asking for more information. I had to look away.

"It's over now." I lay back, folded my arms behind my head, closed my eyes. "Just so you know."

"It's okay, you know. I don't expect you not to have ex-boyfriends." I knew this was meant in a nice way, but I couldn't help feeling that it was really unromantic.

"What about you? What about Amelia?"

"What do you want to know?" I heard the metal cap hit the flask. I shaded my eyes and peered up. He tilted his head back for a quick drink.

"Just normal, basic stuff. Like, how old is she?"

"Twenty-seven."

"Twenty-seven?" I sat up on my elbows.

"Twenty-seven."

"That's old! I'm nineteen! Today!"

"I know. But twenty-seven is only eight years away."

"Well, eight years ago I was eleven," I pointed out. "So it's old."

"Not really." He laughed. "Anyway, she's a lawyer."

"A *lawyer*?" I turned onto my stomach and ran through a quick catalogue in my mind of all the lawyers I knew. Arti's dad was a lawyer. He had a big Mercedes, a comb-over, and bad breath. My aunt Phyllis was a lawyer for criminals. She was always working. Her hair had turned gray early and Mom said it was because her job stressed her out so much. I thought of the lawyers on TV, dazzling judges and juries with their quick tongues. "Like in a courtroom with a judge? Or in an office with a desk?"

"She doesn't actually have a job yet, but she passed the

bar. Anyway, it's over now. Just so you know." He ran a hand down the back of my leg and back up again. I shivered with pleasure. His touch was so light I wasn't entirely sure he was making contact. I stayed really still, hoping he would press a little harder. "The past is the past, you know? That's why I'm glad to make a fresh start."

"So, are you really not moving back to Brooklyn?"

"That's right," he said, and his hand moved to the other leg. "Do you want to go for a swim?"

"Not really." Although I would've said it was impossible, his touch became even lighter as his hand drifted farther up, to the very tops of my thighs, and then, just when I was getting used to it, to the backs of my knees. I dug my toes into the sand.

"Do you want to practice driving again?" he asked.

"Maybe later," I said. His hand was approaching and pulling away and approaching and pulling away. He was tracing, retreating. I wanted to keep the conversation going so he wouldn't stop. "So, if you aren't going back to Brooklyn, where are you going to go?"

"Maybe I'll stay here," he said.

"I think that would be really lonely. Anyplace else?" I rested my cheek on my forearm and breathed in the smell of herbs and spices. The sun warmed my back. My heart beat against the blanket. There was some sort of magnet in his fingertips, because all of my protons, neutrons, and electrons had sparked awake and were following his lead.

"Maybe I'll go to California," he said. "For the surfing. Can you tell what I'm writing?" he asked.

"No."

"I'm writing a message on your leg." I heard the flask open, and the next time his finger touched me, it was cold. "Concentrate." He started on my inner ankle and traveled up to the back of my knee.

Please make this be a long message, I thought, as he continued up my thigh.

"Did you get it?"

"Nope. Try again."

"Okay, I'm going to go bigger and more slowly and in cursive."

"Good idea."

He traced his message again, and my entire body buzzed as he reached the bottom of my bathing suit in what I think was an exclamation point.

"Oh my god," I said, looking up at him, clutching the blanket.

"What? You got it."

"Touch me! Right now!"

He slid his hand inside my bikini and moments later the whole world fractured into color and light, like a kaleidoscope, like all wishes granted at the same time. I rested my head on the sand and heard the heartbeat of the whole world. Or maybe it was just mine. I sighed, laughed, and blinked into the lowering sun.

Thirty-three

"LIZ!" I BURST THROUGH THE DOOR OF THE INN. "LIZ Baxter, where are you?"

"Hiya. Just the girl I'm looking for," Liz said, peeking out from her little reservations closet. "Your surprise is in the kitchen."

"Wait, I need to tell you something." I motioned for her to follow me into the laundry room. "Something's happened to me!"

"It's not another arrest, I hope," Liz said. I shook my head. She wrinkled her nose and leaned closer. "You need a shower, darling. You're a hot mess."

"Yes," I said, taking her hands. "I am a hot mess. Something's happened to me. Something big."

"You did it with the bartender?"

"No," I said. "But it's, um, along those lines. We drove out to some dunes, and. . . ." I fanned myself with my hand and giggled.

"Darling." Her face brightened as she balanced the laundry basket on her hip. "Did he blow your whistle?"

I wasn't exactly sure what she meant. "I think, maybe."

"If he had, you'd know," she said, patting my arm.

"Wait! Then I think he did." I bit my lip.

"So he spun your top, did he? He sounded the alarm? Flipped the switch?"

"Um . . ."

"Did you see the light, darling?"

"Yes!" I jumped. "Yes, I did!"

"Wonderful!"

"It's so wonderful." I leaned against the wall.

"Now, I must warn you." She took hold of my shoulders. "Your body is currently emitting bonding hormones. You mustn't pay too much attention to them. It's just biology. He is not God's gift, no matter what your hormones are telling you. You must promise me that you understand this."

"I can't promise anything." I giggled, sliding down the wall.

"Shall we go tell George?"

"What? George is here?"

"That's my big surprise," she said. "George Gust is in the kitchen."

"George!" I hadn't seen him since last summer, since his book had been published (with my name in it).

"And we have a reservation at Black-Eyed Susan's. Come on, let's tell him."

"Liz, don't you dare."

"But it's such delightful news," she said, laughing her loudest laugh. "I'm sure he'll be very happy for you."

"Liz," I said, showing my most serious face as she hoisted me up. "No."

"George!" Liz said, dragging me into the kitchen. "Here she is!"

"Hi!" I said. In his black T-shirt, faded jeans, and sneakers, George Gust looked almost identical to the way he had the first time I'd met him in this very kitchen and discovered him eating my sandwich, even though he was now a *New York Times* best-selling author.

"Cricket Thompson, faithful intern and birthday girl! I was starting to worry you weren't going to come!"

"Oh, she came!" Liz said, beaming. "She came, George!" My cheeks burned from my hairline to the tips of my ears down to my throat. I shot Liz a look and turned back to George.

"I'm here for a book signing at Mitchell's," he said. "Can you believe it, Cricket? After all that work last summer?"

"I know! And it's great to see you, George, but I've been told I'm a hot mess. So I'm going to go take a shower before dinner. I can't wait to catch up." I turned to go.

"Hurry up," George said. "Our reservation is in fifteen minutes."

George told us about his big news over dinner in the back garden at Black-Eyed Susan's. As we feasted on cold corn soup with chunks of crabmeat and avocado, pan-seared diver scallops, local lettuces with fried green tomatoes, and linguine and quahogs, George told us he had a new book deal, this one about the life of Hillary Clinton. "So many women connect with her," George said. "And there's good reason for it. I'm interested in the psychology of Hillary, her many contradictions and how she's changed the idea of the American woman."

"Is it weird that you're writing this and you're not a woman?" Liz asked, as she helped herself to another glass of the wine. I was sticking to water.

"Not at all," George said. "You wouldn't say that if it were a woman writing about a man, would you?"

Liz considered as she sipped. "No, I suppose not."

"But trust me: my editor and I thought of that. And I have to get this exactly right, because my last book has been so successful. And this advance they gave me? It's no joke. So, I'm under a lot of pressure."

"Are you rich now, George?" Liz asked, eyes popping.

"Let's just say my wife and I were able to make a down payment on an apartment in Park Slope." Liz and I looked at him blankly. "For a journalist, that's basically a miracle. So

I really have to deliver. My career depends on it." He furrowed his brow and he looked a bit pale.

"You just need a female perspective," I said, spearing a scallop. "You know, as you write. And you can interview a lot of women, get a lot of perspectives."

"Exactly," George said, smiling and twirling up a big spoonful of the linguine and quahogs with his fork. "Too bad you'll be busy at Brown, Cricket. I could use you in New York."

I felt a little rush of adrenaline at the idea of myself in a smart-looking dress, walking down a New York street with a notepad under my arm. I thought about Nina and all her New York stories. Maybe I could have my own.

"Brown is a great school," George said. He shook his head, laughing. "What an opportunity. You know, the admissions people at Brown would've laughed their asses off if I'd applied there."

"You don't think you would've gotten in?"

"Not in a million years. Make it a trillion."

"But you're a famous author. I always assumed you went to Yale or Harvard or something." My phone rang. It was a Rhode Island number I didn't recognize, so I ignored the call. It was probably a wrong number. I silenced the phone and placed it on the table.

"In high school I was lot more interested in girls than grades. My SAT scores were a joke. I barely got into CUNY."

"Really?" My whole life had been about getting into

the right college, but here was George, with a shiny new book deal, a best seller on his hands, and a Park Slope apartment, and he hadn't gone anywhere fancy. He was one of the smartest, best people I'd ever met. Did college not actually matter that much?

George twirled up the last of the linguine and threw his napkin on the table. "What do you say: Juice Bar for dessert?"

"Yay! I love the Juice Bar, and Liz will never wait in line with me."

"Some things are worth waiting for, Liz."

"Not tonight. I need to get back for a late check-in. But you two go. I'll see you back at the inn. Thank you for dinner, George. And I'm so happy to finally have a rich friend in New York."

"Don't get carried away," George said as he counted out bills to pay the check. "Come on, Cricket. Let's blow this pop stand." We were halfway out the door when I realized I'd left my phone on the table. I glanced at the screen. The Rhode Island caller had left a voice mail. I'd listen to it later, I thought. Whoever it was, they could wait until after we'd gone to the Juice Bar.

"Maybe I could work for you from Brown," I said to George as we stood in line at the Juice Bar. The late ferry had just come in, and the new arrivals streamed past with their bags over their shoulders, faces lit up with visions of what their time on the island held for them. "I could come to New York on the weekends. I bet I could even find a way to get credit for it."

"There's nothing I'd like more," he said. "You did a great job for me last summer. You have a great attitude. You're smart, fast, and fun to be around. You kept me organized, provided insight, and kept things running smoothly." I beamed at the praise. "But I'm going to need someone full-time. Not just weekends."

"Promise me you'll think about it? I'm going to New York soon anyway," I said as the line moved up and we stepped inside the screen door. "I need to audition for Woody Allen." I hadn't made any concrete plans to do this, but it was on the list and I was going to make it happen somehow.

"Woody Allen? You're an actress now?"

"No, not at all. It's for this, um, project I'm doing."

"What kind of project? For school?"

"No, it's research," I said, studying the menu even though I knew exactly what I was going to order. "Personal research."

George clapped his hand on my shoulder. "That's what I like about you, Thompson. You're always working something out. You're always thinking, always questioning. It's the mark of a good person. And a good journalist."

I made a mental note to stay in touch with George, always.

"So, what's it going to be?" George asked when it was finally our turn to order.

"Chocolate peanut butter, in a waffle cone."

"Make that two," George told the pimply ice-cream scooper as he stuffed a ten-dollar bill in the tip jar.

It wasn't until the next day, when I was getting ready for work, that I listened to the mysterious Rhode Island voice-mail message. I was sitting on the sofa, lacing up my Easy Spirits, when I played it on speaker.

"Hi, Cricket. This is Claudia Gonzales from Brown University admissions. I'm calling with some important information regarding your status. You were admitted with the understanding that you would maintain the exemplary behavior you demonstrated in high school. Our office received some disturbing news regarding an incident on Nantucket. It's crucial that you return my call as soon as possible."

Thirty-four

I HAD A HALF HOUR UNTIL I HAD TO BE AT WORK. I STUFFED my feet into my sneakers and called Claudia Gonzales at the Brown University Admissions Office. I tried her three times, but she didn't answer her phone. I could only leave her a voice mail. I called back and dialed zero to try to reach a human.

"I got a very important message from Ms. Gonzales," I told the girl who picked up. "I need to talk to her."

"It's only me in the office right now," she said. "And I'm just on work study."

"Can I have her cell-phone number? I need to talk to her, like, now."

"Um, I'm not supposed to, um, give out any numbers."

I wanted to reach through the phone and throttle her. "Um, I think I need to go," she said, and hung up.

I flew into the inn's kitchen, where Liz was preparing a salad.

"What's happened now?" she asked.

"I might not get into Brown," I said, my voice rising in panic. "They know that I got shitfaced and broke into Something Natural. They know everything."

"What?"

I played her the voice mail. I was short of breath, studying her face as she listened, hoping that she might have a brilliant British insight or some take on the situation that would mean this was no big deal. But she just shook her head and said, "This is bad, really, really bad."

"I know," I whispered. The panic was climbing back down my throat, clogging my air passages. I sat down and put my head between my knees.

"It was Jules who told them," Liz said.

"We don't know that." I couldn't believe it, but it was the first time the question of who had contacted Brown had entered my mind. Until now, it had just seemed like the all-seeing god of college admissions, the one I'd lived in fear of, to whom I'd prayed with all of my extracurricular activities and made sweet offerings of bright, shiny report cards, was now striking me down out of displeasure.

"Then who was it?" Liz asked. "Do they read the Nantucket police blotter?"

I closed my eyes and placed a hand on my churning stomach. I didn't want to think about it. I tucked in my Breezes T-shirt. "I have to get to work. I need to taste the specials so that I can accurately describe them." As if this were my biggest problem. How was I supposed to recite a speech about wild salmon when my future was in ruins?

Liz put her half-made salad in the fridge and grabbed her keys. "You must talk to this Brown University woman right now. I'll drive. You dial."

"I tried calling Brown," I said, following her out the door. "Claudia Gonzales has gone home for the night."

"Call her at home," Liz said as we climbed into the Jeep. "She must understand what's at stake."

"I don't have her home number. They don't just give home numbers out."

Liz made a show of removing her cell phone from her purse and dialing a number as she started the engine. "Hello, operator? I'm looking for a number in Providence, Rhode Island. A Claudia Gonzales." I handed her the piece of paper on which I'd written her name. "G-O-N-Z-A-L-E-S, as in Sam," Liz raised her eyebrows and nodded. She scribbled on a piece of Cranberry Inn stationery, trying to get the pen to work. "I'll take all three." She spat on the end of her pen and wrote down three numbers.

I called all three Claudia Gonzaleses while Liz drove. The first one didn't speak English, the second sounded like she was a hundred years old; but on the third try I found the Claudia I was looking for.

"How did you get this number?" she asked, sounding too young to be in charge of my life.

"You're listed in information," I said. Liz nodded, as if to confirm that this was totally valid. "I didn't know what to do and I had to talk to you."

"At least you recognize that this is an emergency," she said. I put my hand back on my stomach as it flipped once again, and Claudia Gonzales went on to explain that she'd been sent a video in which I'd identified myself and exhibited behavior that was in no way in line with Brown's code of conduct. Liz watched as I nodded and made notes.

Ms. Gonzales explained that in the next few days I was going to get a certified letter that stated that I had a hearing in a week in front of the Brown Student Conduct Committee. She would be there along with an academic dean, and, because of my place on the team, so would the lacrosse coach. I had one week to prepare an explanation and defend my place at Brown. I jotted down: "video," "one week," "place at Brown," "defend myself."

"We want to know why you did this," she said, "and what your thoughts are upon reflection. We take this kind of thing very seriously."

I wrote "why?" and underlined it twice. After I hung up, I closed my eyes.

"Well?" Liz asked. We were parked in a shaded spot near the restaurant.

"Someone sent them a video of that night at Something Natural."

"Jules! I told you!"

"That doesn't make sense," I said, shaking my head. "We've been so good lately."

"Well, are you still accepted to the university?"

"I have to defend myself," I said. "In some kind of hearing."

"But you're not kicked out?" Liz asked.

"No," I said. "Not yet anyway, but I'm in deep shit."

"Maybe your bartender has some ideas," she said, noticing Ben walking through the back door of the restaurant. She squeezed my khaki knee. I was wearing my ugly thrift-store pants. "In the meantime, we'll both think about how to get you out of this, yeah?"

"So, you have to go on trial? Again?" Ben took my hand in the little alley behind the restaurant. We were hiding out for a few minutes before opening.

"Something like that," I said.

"I don't get it. Who sent the video?"

"I don't know," I said.

"Well, who took it?"

"Jules," I said.

"But she wouldn't send it. It doesn't make sense."

"Have you told your parents?" Ben asked, placing a steadying hand on my lower back.

I shook my head no. I wanted to stay here, in the shelter of his arms, in the alley between Breezes and the Wamp, for as long as possible.

"Honey, I'm so sorry." I never thought I'd like being called "honey" or "sweetie" or any of those names old guys sometimes casually tossed off at the restaurant, but right now, it felt comforting. I leaned against him. For the first time, he felt like my boyfriend. I closed my eyes as those bonding chemicals Liz had warned me about flooded my bloodstream.

"So, what's your plan?" asked Ben.

"I'm going to do what I always do," I said.

"What's that?"

"Fight like hell." Behind Ben, a nighthawk looped through the sky, searching for dinner. Dad used to point out their long, pointed wings on our bike rides on summer evenings in Providence.

"You're one tough girl," he said.

"I'm an attack wing," I said. "In lacrosse."

"And in life," Ben said, as he kissed the top of my head. "Sadie's going off island for a few days tomorrow. You can stay with me if you want."

"I'd like that," I said. His arms felt strong and protective. Older.

"We'd better get back in there. Tonight's going to be a nightmare. We're booked solid."

Ben was right. That night we didn't have one rush or two rushes. The whole shift was a rush. What everyone said was true. August was the busiest, craziest time of all. I made more mistakes than usual. A lady who'd ordered the lobster roll with butter got it with mayonnaise. A fat-fingered man who'd wanted the bluefish wound up with the snapper. But their complaining looks and sharp words barely registered, and thankfully, even Karla was too busy acting as both hostess and busboy, and even hopping behind the bar at one point, to notice. I kept thinking about Claudia Gonzales's words and that video. I barely remembered it, but I could picture Jules filming Zack and me and telling us to put our arms around each other.

As I bused a table, gathering dirty glasses and dessert dishes onto a tray, another memory came back to me: of Jules flinching when I told her about Nina's life list. I dumped the glasses and plates at the dish-washing station, realizing that Jules's sending the video to Brown was another version of what had happened last year, when I'd spoken at her mother's memorial service. Jules had been very angry, but instead of telling me like a normal person, she had lashed out.

I headed back to the dining room and saw that Karla had seated my whole section again. Six new tables at once. I barely had time to breathe.

At the end of the night, after I'd counted out over three hundred dollars in tips, and just as I was about to clean the cappuccino machine, which was particularly milk-encrusted and sticky, I got a text from Jules: Hey, Misdemeanors. It's me, Crimes. Come over tomorrow? We can watch those Woody Allen movies. It's supposed to rain.

Was this what she was going to do? I thought as I wiped down the metal grate on the stupid cappuccino machine. She'll just let me go down in flames and think that I would never suspect her?

I turned on the milk steamer, not realizing the nozzle was aimed right at my hand. The steam seared my skin in a hissing blast. I ran to the sink and let cold water run over the distinct band of red, which was swelling and blistering, marking my hand like lashes of a whip.

Thirty-five

"LOOK WHAT I HAVE," JULES SAID, OPENING THE FRONT door of the Claytons' house the next morning. I didn't step inside, even though it was cold and wet where I stood. According to my iPhone, it was already raining, but I stood in the misting air, arms crossed, careful not to touch the place on my hand that had burned. Even though I'd let the icy cold water run over it for several minutes last night, it was still too tender to touch.

Minutes before, I had been on the phone with Coach Stacy, who told me, among other things, that she was extremely disappointed that I'd mentioned on the video that I hadn't been keeping up with my training. Not only was she sitting on the committee at the hearing, but also, her decision would be based on how I performed at a scrimmage at the training camp she was running at St. Timothy's. I would be expected to be there the day before the hearing for the camp's closing scrimmage, to demonstrate that I was up to the task of playing at the college level.

Jules was holding the door open with her foot, not picking up on my vibes. She displayed three Woody Allen DVDs, running a hand over them as if I'd just won them on a game show. "I have *Manhattan*, *Annie Hall*, and *Hannah and Her Sisters*. I also have *Crimes and Misdemeanors*, but then I thought, nah, too soon." She laughed, but her face fell when she registered my stony expression and crossed arms. She wrinkled her nose and said, "Are you going to come in or what?"

"Just tell me why."

"Why what?" Jules stepped outside, tucking the DVDs under her arm.

"This is because I didn't tell you about the list I found on the back of your mom's picture, isn't it? Or is this about last year? You still haven't forgiven me. You're never going to forgive me, are you?"

"What the fuck are you talking about?" When she lied, she pursed her lips and didn't make eye contact. Her mouth was hanging open, and she wasn't even blinking. "I'm not mad about the list. I stayed up last night digging through boxes to find these." She held up the DVDs. "I wanted to watch them with you. Maybe it's you who hasn't forgiven me. Ever thought of that?"

"Then who sent the video?"

"What video?"

"Of us getting drunk and breaking into Something Natural? Someone sent it to Brown, and now I might not get in. I have a hearing in a week with an academic dean, the head of admissions, and the lacrosse coach. And not only that, but the lacrosse coach saw me saying I hadn't been keeping up with my training. I have to prove myself in a scrimmage. If I don't do well, I don't get her vote."

"Are you serious? Jesus, Cricket," Jules said. "ZACK, GET OUT HERE!" Despite the obvious fact that he'd been there too, I hadn't even considered the idea that he might have sent it. He couldn't have. He was my first love. First loves don't do that.

"Don't give me that look," Jules said to me. "He took the video, not me." She was right. Jules had only held the camera for a moment. It was Zack's phone. It was his idea.

"Why do you have to yell?" Zack asked as he emerged from the house holding a bowl of cereal. He was wearing just his Hanover soccer shorts. I studied his perfect torso, his sweet features, and his hair, rumpled from sleeping. "Hey, Cricket," he said with a soft smile.

"You know that video you took of us?" Jules asked.

"What video?" Zack asked, eating his Cheerios.

"You took a video that night," Jules said. "At Something Natural."

"Oh, yeah," he said, remembering. "I did."

"Did you send it to Brown?" Jules asked.

"Why the hell would I do that?"

"Someone sent that video to Brown and now I might not get in," I said.

"What?" Zack paused in midbite. "I would never do that."

I wanted to believe him so badly.

"You were passed out all night," Jules said. "Maybe you did it when you were passed out."

"I couldn't even find my way home; you think I could locate the e-mail address of someone in the admissions office at Brown?"

"Someone sent that video," I said.

"Take us through what happened that night," Jules said to Zack.

"I took the thermoses from Jules," Zack said, "and I started walking, and I remember getting really disoriented and lying down in the park and telling myself I was camping."

"That has nothing to do with anything. When did you wake up?" Jules asked.

"I woke up because my phone was ringing," Zack said. "It was light out by then."

"Who was it?" I asked.

"Parker," Zack said. "She came and got me."

"We're so dumb," Jules said. "Get me your phone."

"Screw you."

"Go!"

Zack went inside and came back with his phone. Jules snatched it from him and opened his sent mail folder. She scrolled until she found what she was looking for: an e-mail to the Brown University Admissions Office, with a video attachment. It had been sent on my birthday.

"I swear I didn't send it."

"No shit," I said. "Your girlfriend did."

He closed his eyes. "I'm so sorry." I held my breath, waiting for something else, but he just shook his head.

"Sorry? Sorry is not good enough," I said. "It's not even close."

He covered his face with his hands.

I felt a shard of glass lodge in my heart. "You're not even going to break up with her, are you?"

"Shit," he said.

"You really have changed. You know that?"

"Um, do you guys want me to leave?" Jules asked.

"Yes," Zack said.

"No," I said.

She froze.

"This is all going to work out," Zack said. "It has to."

"What are you talking about, it has to work out? No, it doesn't. I'm not a senator's daughter. I can't just snap my fingers and have my troubles go away. This is my life, Zack. My life! Everything I've ever worked for!"

"Cricket," Zack said. "I'm so, so sorry."

"Stop saying that. Sorry doesn't help me."

"I'll help you," he said, breathless. "I'll fix it."

"How?" I asked. He said nothing. "Guess what, Zack? While you were busy protecting Parker, she ruined my life."

"Cricket, please."

"I never want to talk to you again," I said and took off.

"Wait," Jules said, catching up to me. It had really started to rain now. Jules wasn't wearing shoes. Her toes were red against the pavement. "We're going to make sure you get back in."

"Can you admit Parker is a mean girl now? I just want to hear you admit it. I want you to say it. I want to know that you're on my side."

"I'm on your side," she said. "But Parker is severely troubled—"

"No, no, no. Fuck 'troubled,'" I said and ran away, fast enough so that even someone wearing shoes couldn't have caught me.

Thirty-six

I RODE MY BIKE TO SADIE'S COTTAGE IN THE RAIN. WITH the exception of some hard-core bicyclists decked out in spandex, I was the only one on the path. The rain had quieted the island, filling the air with the scent of wet grass and cooling pavement, urging people indoors to board games and sweaters. But I was racing my own thoughts on the way to 'Sconset. *I choose Ben over Zack,* I told myself as I whirred past Polpis Road. *I will write over the story of Zack with the story of Ben. I will take my heart in my own hands.*

By the time I arrived, the muscles in my legs were tingling, my hands were cold, and I was soaked to the bone. When Ben opened the screen door, he looked like the perfect picture of a hot summer boy. He stood framed in the warm light of the cottage, barefoot in an old Sarah Lawrence

T-shirt and jeans. He smiled and I stepped inside the house, rain dripping from my hair onto the hooked rug with the Sankaty lighthouse on it. He was playing an old-fashioned record on an actual record player. His guitar was out of its case, leaning against the fireplace.

"You look like a drowned rat," he said. I frowned. "A cute rat," he added. He handed me a T-shirt and sweatpants from his makeshift dresser next to the sofa. "Go change. I'll make you an Irish coffee."

"That sounds perfect," I said. After my fight with Zack and Jules and the rainy ride to 'Sconset, an Irish coffee felt like the most civilized, exquisite thing known to human-kind. I took the clothes from him and headed into the bathroom. Though, what was the point? I wondered as I shut the door behind me. I wasn't planning on staying dressed for long.

I took off my wet clothes and hung them on the towel rack. I looked in the mirror and shook out my damp hair. I was about to pull on the sweatpants, but I paused and left them folded by the sink. My cheeks were pink from the ride over. I searched my eyes for evidence of tears, splashed a little water on my face, and dabbed on some lip gloss.

"Well, hello, there, pantless one," Ben said, as I stepped out of the bathroom.

"They were way too big." I shrugged, took the Irish coffee and sat on the sofa, stretching my legs out.

"So," he said, sitting next to me. "Did you talk to Jules?" I nodded. "And?"

"And Zack." The name had an electric charge. It shocked my mouth.

"I meant, AND what did she say? Did she send the video?"

"No. That other girl did. Parker."

"Ah," Ben said. He nodded. "Zack's girlfriend, right?" I didn't like the sound of his name on Ben's tongue, and I'd never, ever get use to the phrase *Zack's girlfriend*.

"I don't want to talk about them," I said, sipping my Irish coffee. It was strong and a little bitter. "I'm going to add a little more sugar to this. Not quite sweet enough."

"Don't be long," Ben said as I headed toward the kitchen. "You look good in my T-shirt, but I think you'd look even better without it."

"Where's the sugar?" I asked, searching the cupboards.

"In the cupcake," he said.

"Oh, okay." I spied the ceramic cupcake and set about looking for a spoon.

"Maybe we should go surfing later. I bet the waves are awesome right now," Ben said. As I searched for a spoon, he went on talking, about surfing before a storm. I opened a drawer and found what Mom would have called the "catch-all"—the place where one kept keys, gum, coupons, and take-out menus. Staring up at me was a picture of Ben kissing a girl with dark hair sitting under a CONGRATS! banner on the front porch. Amelia, I thought. I picked it up and studied it. I had always pictured her fair, like Ben and me, but I'd been wrong. She had dark hair and olive skin. I caught my breath as I realized who she was. Her hair was longer in this picture, and her body was a little more ample than it was now, but there was no mistaking the thin band of a tattoo around her arm, or her high, distinctive cheekbones.

"Ben?" I said, stepping out into the living room with the picture in my hand, interrupting his monologue on currents and storms. "Were you engaged to Amy? Is Amy Amelia?"

A full five seconds passed before he spoke. "I didn't know how to tell you." He reddened. He bit his lip.

"I feel like such an idiot," I said. "Why didn't you tell me? Why did you lie?"

"Everything I told you was true. I was engaged. She cheated on me. I came to Nantucket to start over."

"You left out a pretty important detail."

"I told her it was over, but I couldn't stop her from coming out here and getting a job. Karla's her aunt."

"Why didn't you get a job somewhere else?"

"Bartending jobs are hard to find on Nantucket."

"That hard? So hard you have to work with your ex-fiancée?"

"Actually, yes. And it's not like you told me everything about your past."

"Me?" I put a hand on my chest. "What did I hide?"

"That you're still in love with Zack?"

"I am not!" I said, hoping that if I said the words, they'd be true.

"Cricket, you should see your face when you say his name." Ben's eyes were liquid with compassion. "It takes one to know one."

"You're still in love with Amelia? I mean Amy, whatever her real name is."

He covered his face with his hands and sighed. "I don't know. But she did break my heart. And I don't think I'm going to get over it for a long time."

"Then what are we doing together?" I swallowed, trying to make sense of the situation. "What have we been doing all summer?"

"Having fun? Helping each other move on?"

I inhaled sharply. "You were using me."

"Hey, that's not true," Ben said. "Not any more than you were using me."

I stared at the wooden floor, speechless. Was he right? Had I been using him, too? I headed to the bathroom to change. He followed me, but I closed the door on him.

"You don't have to go, Cricket. I like you and I think you like me," he said through the door as I took off his shirt. "Not everything fits in a neat little box. Not every relationship needs a label. Let's just surrender and enjoy each other."

"That sounds like a pile of crap." My skin goose-pimpled as I put on my cold, rain-soaked clothes.

"Sometimes you just have to let go," he said.

"I have to get out of here," I said. I handed him his clothes and jammed my feet into my wet sneakers.

"At least let me drive you?" Ben said, but I was already out the door.

I pedaled back toward town. I thought about that picture of Sadie dancing on the beach and wondered why I couldn't be more like her. Sadie herself said that at my age she'd just wanted to have fun and get laid, and it had seemed cool when she said it. So why did I have to care so much about what things meant? Why couldn't I just enjoy this hot older surfer guy who turned me on like crazy? And I wasn't like Nina, either. I wasn't a rich Park Avenue girl with a penchant for art and high culture. I was just a middle-class kid who had blown her chance at an Ivy League education.

As the sun ripped through the cloud layer, a deep anger swelled inside me. I was angry with Ben and Amy and even Karla, for keeping me in the dark. I was angry with myself. I had allowed myself to take my eye off the ball. I knew better. I was angry at Jules for letting me get that drunk when she knew I had no experience with alcohol. I was angry at Zack for protecting Parker. And I was enraged at Parker for being so cavalier with my life. But none of this surprised me.

What surprised me was that I was angry at Nina. I was angry at her for loving me when she was alive in a way that made me feel like I was one of her own. I was pissed that she had lived long enough to let me believe that I could be like her, but hadn't hung around long enough to show me how. Instead, she had left me with a list of rich-girl fantasies that I could only pretend to actualize. She'd filled my head with dreams of places I couldn't really go. I wouldn't be able to go to Paris or Italy until I was grown-up, with a job of my own. And then I wouldn't be able to do it with the style and insouciance that she had had. That wasn't something you could earn through hard work and scholarships. It was something you were born with. She was the reason I had come out to this stupid island, and I hated her for it. My mom had been right last year. I *had* worshiped Nina, and it *was* silly and useless, and, worst of all, it was probably even tacky.

When I got back to the manager's apartment, I took the picture of Nina off the wall. I was going to rip it up. My hands were poised and ready to tear when I saw a pile of Woody Allen DVDs, tied up with a ribbon, sitting on my sofa bed with a note from Jules.

Hey, Miss Demeanors!

You forgot your DVDs. I found them for you. We're going to fight this. We're going to get you back into Brown. I promise. AND I love you forever! Love, Miss Crimes.

P.S.: Got to get you in shape for the coach. Your lacrosse training starts tomorrow at 9 a.m. sharp! See you then.

P.P.S.: Start with Manhattan. *It was Mom's favorite, since she went to the same school as the girl in the movie.*

Jules had sealed it with a lipstick kiss. She'd even drawn a bunch of funny pictures of us. There was one of us playing lacrosse. There was one of me standing on her back crawling through the window of Something Natural. There was one of us swimming at night, our boobs floating to the surface under a full moon. As angry as I was, I had to laugh. What if Jules had been right when she said that I was the one who had been unable to forgive her for last summer? What if I was the one holding on to anger? What if Ben was right about my needing to let go?

I released the photo of Nina from my closed fist. I took three deep breaths, smoothed it out, and hid it in a secret pocket on the inside of my suitcase. Then I picked up the phone and did what I'd been dreading doing.

"Hello?" Mom's voice was chipper, happy to hear from me out of the blue. I imagined her in her Cape Cod T-shirt and running shorts, her heavy, golden hair falling in front of her face as she reached for the phone.

"It's me," I said. I took a deep breath and gathered my courage. "There's something I need to tell you."

Thirty-seven

THE CONVERSATION LASTED ALMOST AN HOUR. SHE TOOK the phone into her bedroom so that Brad wouldn't overhear. He had officially moved in. I talked her through what happened scene by scene. For the first time in my life, her voice offered me no comfort. Each "What?" was hard as concrete, and each silence was as cold as March rain.

"You're going to get back in, right?" Mom asked when I'd finished by telling her about my conversation with Claudia Gonzales. "I mean, she said you were going to get back into Brown, didn't she?"

"I don't know, Mom. That's the whole thing. I don't know. That's why I have a hearing next Monday. Weren't you listening?" It had been painful enough to go over the details with her once. I filled a glass with tap water and drank it down.

"Well, you'll just have to get a waitressing job here. It will have to be someplace you can walk to, because you won't have a car. You'll have to take classes at the community college. Maybe pick up some babysitting work."

"Stop it, Mom," I said. The picture she was painting had me on the verge of tears. I had known she was going to be pissed off, but I hadn't expected this.

"This is going to be your reality, Cricket. And mine, too. This is not what I imagined for myself, either, you know. I had started to get used to the idea of starting over, just Brad and me. But it's too late to do anything else, isn't it? How could you do this to yourself?"

"I don't know, Mom, okay? Haven't you ever made a mistake?"

"Oh, I've made plenty. But this isn't about me. This is about you. And this story you've told me about getting wasted and breaking into a café? Jesus, it doesn't even sound like you, Cricket. Is this who you are now?"

"I don't know, Mom," I said. "I don't know who I am right now." These might have been the truest words I'd ever spoken, and there was at least some calm in that.

"Have you told your father yet?"

"Tomorrow," I said. I was dreading telling Dad. Snippets of the speech he had given at my graduation party kept coming back to me. The stuff about how he couldn't be prouder of me, and the part about how they'd placed a bet on me, putting all of their money into my education, and hit the jackpot when I got into Brown. I thought of how they'd sold the minivan; I thought of the extra mortgages, the bank loans, and the vacations they hadn't taken. Their sacrifices stared me down.

"So, you don't want to upset him, but you'll upset me?" Mom asked.

"Well, you're . . . my mom," I said.

"Yes, I am." She sighed. "I have to work in the morning and I don't know how I'm going to fall asleep tonight. I'm going to have to take a pill."

I knew those pills. They were small and blue, and she'd taken them every night in the year after the divorce.

"Mama?"

"What?"

"I'm sorry." I curled myself around a pillow. "I'm really, really sorry."

"I know you are, baby." She sighed again. "I know."

I debated calling Dad, but I couldn't. I would do it tomorrow. I took a hot shower, then I watched *Manhattan* on the old TV in the manager's apartment. I pulled the blankets up under my chin as the images of a big city flickered across the screen: a crowded deli; a bakery; that museum with the wide, swirling staircase; the awning of a fancy hotel; an enormous bridge over a black river; a candlelit bistro. It seemed so enchanting and foreign and far away.

Thirty-eight

"WAKE UP, SPORTY!"

I blinked awake to see Liz smiling down at me in what looked like her version of workout clothes: a tank top with hot pink bra straps peeking out; cutoffs; and a pair of slip-on sneakers that were meant for skateboarding.

"What?" I glanced at the clock. It was eight a.m. I'd only had a few hours of sleep.

"The muffins are made, the girls have the inn under control, and we need to work out. Need to get you back in shape, don't we? Come on," she said, pulling me up to a sitting position. "Get moving."

"You're going to work out with me?"

"I'm going to damned well try. It's about time I lost some weight. Wine and cookies add up." She grabbed the flesh around her middle and jiggled it. I laughed. "Oh, you laugh, but by the time we get you back into Brown, I'm going to look like Pippa Middleton." She sucked in her stomach and struck a pose.

"Liz, I only have a week. Six days now."

"Then we'd better get working, hadn't we? Up you go. Get on your trainers. We're going to go for a run. Look, I even brought you breakfast." One of her famous cranberry-orange muffins sat on a napkin on the coffee table next to a steaming cup of coffee. "You're going to need fuel. We should run at least a mile. Maybe two."

"Okay," I said, not having the heart to tell her that a mile wasn't very far at all.

There was a knock at the door. I turned to see Jules's face pressed up against the window.

"Her!" Liz said, narrowing her eyes and grabbing Gavin's rain stick from the closet. She shook it menacingly as she opened the door. "You're not welcome here!"

"Jules didn't send it," I said, jumping in front of Jules. "Liz! She wants to help me. It wasn't her. I promise."

"Were you going to hit me with that?" Jules asked, holding her lacrosse stick in front of her face in self-defense.

"Yes," Liz said, raising the rain stick up like a baseball bat, "and I still might."

"Liz, she has nothing to do with it." I seized the rain stick.

"Do you have proof?" Liz's eyes were wild behind her thickly mascaraed lashes.

"Yes," I said. "We found the video attached to an e-mail sent from her brother's account."

"Zack sent the movie? Bastard! They're all bastards, the lot of 'em."

"It was my brother's girlfriend, Parker," Jules said. The word *girlfriend* landed like a brick. Jules met my eyes. "His *mean, nasty* girlfriend."

"Is this true?" Liz asked me. "Parker sent it? The Carmichael girl?"

"A hundred percent," I said.

"Shady family, they are," Liz said.

"Now that we've narrowly avoided an assault," Jules said, "are you ready to work out, Cricket?"

"Actually, we were just about to go for a run," Liz said.

"I was going to . . ." Jules started, but I cut her off.

"We're all going running together," I said.

"I say we go to Altar Rock," Jules said as she stretched her hamstrings.

"But that's miles away," Liz said.

"That's kind of the point," Jules said. "Cricket needs to get her endurance up."

I put a hand on Liz's shoulder. "Head home whenever you feel like it."

We were barely out of town when Liz, red-faced and panting, said, "Tell you what, mates. I think I've exerted myself enough for today. I'll go home, get some refreshments, and meet you at the rock. In the car."

"You did well for your first run, Liz," I said, jogging in place. "You'll go a little farther each day." It was a Miss Kangism.

Liz headed back toward the inn. Jules and I picked up the pace. Even though I was a faster sprinter, we were pretty evenly matched when it came to distance.

"What's up with Ben?" Jules asked.

"We broke up yesterday. I don't really want to talk about it." Could I even call it breaking up if we'd never actually been together?

"Rough day," she said. "I'm sorry."

"It's okay. How's Jay?"

"Awesome," she said. Out of my peripheral vision, I could see her beaming. I had a weird premonition that they might get married one day, even though it had been Jay's and my wedding that we'd joked about back before everything happened with Zack. "I'm going to see him in Boston on Friday, and I'm staying for a few nights. I can't wait, if you know what I mean." She meant sex.

"And what's going on with your dad?" I asked, changing the subject.

"Still officially single," she said, and we high-fived.

Several miles later, after Liz had passed us in her car, with the radio blaring, Jules pointed down a dirt road, and we followed it toward what looked like a water tower. We'd been running for another five minutes or so when she said, "Race you to the top of the rock!"

Ahead of us, Liz waved. She was shouting something at us, but I couldn't understand her. The wind was swirling in my ears as I put all of my frustration and anger into the last one hundred yards, leaving Jules in my actual dust.

"Jesus, you're fast," Jules said when she reached the top seconds after I did and we collapsed in a heaving, sweaty pile. I pulled out my iPhone and checked the pedometer. Five miles. My face was burning up. I was happy to see Liz and her gallon of fresh lemonade.

"Well done," Liz said, pouring us each a cupful.

I drank it all in three swallows. "Thank you," I said, savoring the sweet, tart liquid. "Liz, you are the best."

"This is awesome," Jules said, as she tossed back her second cup and went for a third.

The top of this rock was the highest point I'd ever been to on Nantucket. I could see a scalloped harbor. A stretch of low, rugged land. In the distance were scattered several shingled houses, and beyond them lay a faint stroke of ocean. My phone rang. "It's my dad."

"Get it," Jules said.

"I can't. I can't tell him."

"You have to," Liz said. And when I didn't make a move, she leveled a stern look at me. "Cricket, now."

I answered the phone. "Hi, Dad." I said, and held my breath. I put the phone to my ear and walked several paces away from the girls.

"Your mom called me this morning," Dad said. "She told me what happened. Sweetheart, what are you going to do?" His sympathetic tone surprised me.

"Just tell me that you're mad," I said, gazing out at that small harbor, so perfect it looked like a painting, with three sailboats gliding across it. "Tell me how disappointed you are."

"Yes, I'm disappointed. But I'm more worried," he said. "This could be one of those big mistakes."

"Sometimes it feels like everyone's allowed to make mistakes but me."

He laughed.

"What?"

"I'm laughing because it's true. If there's ever been a model student, a model kid, it's you. But as far as mistakes go, you picked a big one."

"Did you ever make a big mistake?" I asked. My chin was trembling.

"Did I tell you about the time I failed my only daughter?"

My throat tightened. I closed my eyes. "No."

"There were so many times I should have been there for you and I wasn't. You were always so on top of things that I didn't think you needed me. But every girl needs her dad. I didn't ask you to be in my wedding. I devoted all of my time to my new marriage. Not getting into college? That seems like small potatoes when I think about my mistakes."

"You didn't fail me, Dad," I said, as I mangled the branch of an innocent shrub. "I failed myself."

"But when you came to me last summer, and you were

so angry, I should've talked to you then. I shouldn't have let you leave that house."

I wiped away tears. Last summer, he had pretty much ignored my eighteenth birthday but thrown a hoedown for his stepchild, Alexi, who was turning six.

"I don't think I was a very good party guest," I said.

"I should've wrapped my arms around you," Dad said. "I should've told you that I loved you, sweetie. You needed me, and I wasn't there. And I'm sorry."

"I need you now," I said quietly.

"I'm here."

"I have this hearing and I have no idea what I'm going to say. I'm going to have to write a speech and explain to the coach. I can't say that I was just being stupid. But that's what it was. I was being stupid. At the wrong time and in the wrong place."

"Well, why did you do it?" he asked. "Why did you get drunk and break into a sandwich shop?"

"I was working so hard," I said. "I hadn't had a real day off since I got here."

"You haven't really had a day off since you started high school," Dad said. "But you've never done anything like this before. So, I ask you again, why?"

Why *had* I done this? I'd had a perfect opportunity to get drunk and be rebellious with Jules before the summer began, at Jay's house, when everyone was going to break into the secret Brown bowling alley. But I hadn't wanted it then. So what had changed?

"I found this list," I said. I hadn't been able to tell Mom about Nina's list. She resented Nina. I knew it would've made her sympathize with me less, not more.

"What list?"

I told Dad about Nina's picture, about Rodin and Paris, about driving a stick shift. I told him about Sadie and the photos of people dancing on the beach. I told him about Campari and the Amalfi Coast with Alison Huang. Dad listened on the other line, saying, *"Uh-huh,"* and *"Hmm."*

"Nina went to Brown, didn't she?" he asked.

"Yes," I said.

"You know, it's not every student who gets a list like that and does that kind of research. It took creativity and passion and some original thinking. Sounds like Brown material to me."

I felt space open up inside me. The light of possibility. The glow of hope.

"You're right," I said. I would use the list to defend myself. I would tell the story of how I'd followed it as an example of why I was exactly Brown material. "Are you going to tell Rosemary and Jim?"

"Do you want me to?"

"No," I said. "Not unless we have to."

"Then I won't tell," he said.

"You won't tell Polly?" I asked. I held my breath.

"I won't tell a soul," he said. "And let me know if you need help. I am an English professor, you know."

"Thanks, Dad."

I climbed back up the rock where Jules and Liz were sunning themselves like lizards.

"I'm going to use the list to defend myself," I told them, as I poured myself another big cup of lemonade. "I'm going to go through it and explain how I followed each step and how it led me to the moment at Something Natural."

"That's perfect," Jules said, propping herself up on her elbow.

"Actually, that's brilliant," Liz said. "You can talk about how you wish to take art classes about Rodin."

"And a class about the history of the car?" Jules said.

"You think they offer 'the history of the car' at Brown?" I asked.

"Why not?" Jules shrugged.

"Anyway, it's all true," I said. "It's not bullshit."

"This means you have to go to New York now," Jules said, "to learn about Woody Allen."

"I can just watch the DVDs," I said. "I can watch them until I draw some meaning from them."

Liz squinted into the sun. "But that's a place you can actually go."

"Besides," Jules said. "I don't know what you're going to learn from watching *Manhattan*. It's really creepy how he dates that young girl."

"What about the last thing on the list?" I asked.

"There was another thing?" Jules asked, sitting up straight.

"Oh, yeah, I didn't tell you," I said. "It was 'See Saint Francis from altar.' I figure it was something she wanted to see on her wedding day."

"Cricket. We're at Altar. Right now. This is Altar Rock."

"Is Saint Francis a church?" I asked. "Is it a church you can see from here?"

"I have no idea," Jules said. "I'll ask Dad."

I took another look around. I felt so close to the sky. I could see for miles. I could see that glistening, pristine harbor; fields of low, green shrubs forked by winding, sandy paths; a pale stripe of ocean. But no churches, no crosses, no saints.

Thirty-nine

"WHAT'S HAPPENED NOW, THOMPSON?" KARLA ASKED WHEN I knocked on the door of her office. She was looking over purchase orders and working out some numbers on an old-fashioned adding machine. "Did you rob a bank?"

"Not funny," I said. "I'm here to get my paycheck."

"It's in here somewhere." She handed me the stack of envelopes with staff names written on them. I paused when I saw Amy's full name—Amelia Garcia—then continued on to find mine.

"How come no one told me Ben and Amy used to be engaged?"

"Why would that be a topic of conversation?" Karla said, looking up. "Especially since there's nothing going on between you two?" She raised an eyebrow. I shrugged. "Love and business do not mix. Trust me."

"But you hired her after you hired Ben?"

"She happens to be my favorite niece. I've never been able to say no to that girl. Anyway, I don't see how this is your business. Is there something else you need? I'm kinda busy." She gestured to her piles of paperwork.

"Yeah. I'm just confirming that I have Saturday, Sunday, and Monday off." I needed to be back in Rhode Island on Saturday in order to be well rested and ready for the scrimmage at nine a.m. on Sunday, and Monday was my hearing at Brown. "Because of my mistake? I mentioned it last week?"

Karla spun around on her office chair to check the schedule hanging on the wall. "I've got you covered for the weekend, but you have to figure out Monday."

"But I told you—"

"Ask Amy. She's off, although she'll have had a really tough weekend. Being down a waitress in August is no joke."

It occurred to me I could just quit at the end of the week. If I was lucky enough to still be attending college, I had seven thousand in the bank, and I could probably make another grand in my next four or five shifts. But I'd promised Karla that I would work through the end of August, and she'd been so nice to not fire me after my arrest that I didn't want to break that promise.

"Amy's the only one?"

"Better say pretty please," Karla said as I left her office. "With sugar on top."

Amy was sitting at the bar refilling salt shakers. All of her behavior now made sense. Trying to get rid of me. Her high fever of emotions. Her lipstick and mascara.

"Amy, I have a favor to ask."

"What is it?" She didn't look up as she poured a steady stream of salt into the delicate, silver-topped shaker, then tapped it to shake off the excess.

"I'm wondering if there's any chance you can cover for me on Monday?"

"After that weekend of double shifts? No frickin' way. I'm going to the beach."

"Please." I sat on the barstool next to her and faced her. "It's really important. I need that time if I want to get back into college. It's my one chance to correct the mistake I made. Imagine making one mistake that had the potential to ruin your life."

"I don't need to imagine," she said, screwing on the top of one saltshaker and reaching for another. Maybe it was because of her small stature, but until Ben told me that she was also Amelia, I had thought Amy was my age. Now that I really looked at her, I could see some fine lines around her eyes. I could see long nights in the library and the broken engagement. I could see that she was twenty-seven.

"Because you cheated on Ben?"

She turned to me with fanned fingers and anxious eyes. "He told you?"

"I found a picture."

"He has a picture? What picture? Where is it?"

"I found it at Sadie's house. I think it's from your engagement party."

"He took you to Sadie's?" Her chest caved. Her eyes webbed with red.

"We're not together anymore," I said.

"Oh!" She gasped with relief. The lines around her eyes softened. "What happened?"

"He's not over you."

"Did he say that?"

"Basically."

"I love him so much," she said, hiding her face. "I just got freaked out, you know? It was one stupid night. I turned down an internship to come here and try to get him back, but he met you."

"He doesn't love me," I said, reaching over the bar to grab a cocktail napkin. I handed it to her and she dabbed her eyes. It was true. No matter which way I'd dissected it, I'd come to the same conclusion. He liked me. He liked teaching me how to surf and how to drive stick. He liked playing the guitar for me and building fires by the ocean while I watched, soft with awe. And I'm pretty sure he enjoyed making me feel like a firecracker on the Fourth of July in the dunes of the nature preserve. I guess if you've had an older girlfriend for a while, it would feel good to be the one who knows something for a change, but it didn't make his heart any more available, and there's just no substitute for someone's heart.

"He's here," I said, watching Ben walk through the door with his earbuds in. As he took in the two of us huddled by the bar, his pace slowed. He looked genuinely nervous.

"Don't tell him I cried," she whispered as she hopped off the stool.

"I won't. Are you going to cover for me on Monday?"

"Yeah, fine." She pushed the tray of saltshakers toward me. "Finish these while I go fix my makeup."

"What was that about?" Ben asked as he stepped behind the bar. "Or should I even ask?"

"Amy's going to cover for me on Monday," I said.

"That's it?" Ben asked, setting up his cutting board and knife.

"I told her I knew," I said, taking over the salt duties. "She really loves you, you know." Ben seemed unmoved as he rinsed off lemons and limes. I wiped the extra salt from the rim of the small container with my finger.

"She cheated on me after I proposed to her. That's one of those actions that crosses a line. I just don't think there's any going back after that. Not for me, anyway." Amy emerged from the ladies' room with a fresh layer of bright red lipstick, and my heart broke for her. She was going to wear herself out trying to get him back. "I'm sorry she's sad, but I was straight up with her. She followed me here anyway."

"You're tough," I said.

"Says the attack wing. Hey," he said, touching my hand. "Are we friends?"

"Sure," I said. "I don't have any guy friends."

"You do now. So, do you want to know how to make a perfect martini? It's a skill that comes in surprisingly handy."

For the next five days I was on a strict schedule. Every night I worked at Breezes. Things were always a little awkward with Ben and Amy for the first half hour, but we were too slammed for them to stay weird. Amy was a lot nicer to me now that Ben and I weren't together. She whispered funny remarks to me about the customers, delivered drinks for me when I was in the weeds, and even took over a table of jerks for me. The busy nights, I went home with at least two hundred and fifty dollars. It all went straight into my bank account. When I reached eight thousand, on Thursday night, I sent an e-mail to Rosemary and Jim.

Every morning, Jules and I worked out. We ran to Altar Rock. We ran to Surfside. We ran to Cisco. We practiced ground balls and shots on goal in the fields of Nantucket High School.

"You know what I want more than anything?" I asked, collapsing in the sand after a workout that had ended with a game of catch at Children's Beach. "A sandwich from Something Natural."

"I don't think we're welcome there," Jules said, laughing.

"They probably have our pictures in the back." I laughed. "Nantucket's Most Wanted."

"Let's go to the Juice Bar, where they don't know about our criminal history."

"Hey," I said as she grabbed my hands and pulled me up. "Did Zack break up with Parker?"

"Not yet. But don't give up on him, Cricket."

"It's too late." It was like Ben said. There were some things that you couldn't go back from.

"When it comes to love, it's never too late. Come on," she said, dusting the sand off her butt. "Let's think of what you'll say in this letter to Woody Allen."

"Do you think he'll actually let me audition if he knows the whole story?"

"You never know," Jules said. "Hey, have you ever had a watermelon cream from the Juice Bar? You have to try one. They were my mom's favorite."

Later, when I was writing my letter to Woody Allen, explaining Nina's life list and my mission to reenact it, Zack called. I didn't pick up. If he chose to stay with someone who would do what she had done to me, he didn't love me. He called twice more, but I didn't answer. I deleted the voice mails without listening to them. Liz found the address of Woody Allen's agent. I mailed the letter on my way to work.

Every day, I worked on my presentation. I pored over the Brown Web site and wrote down what they were looking for in a student: inspired, talented, motivated, creative, resourceful, committed, independent. I focused on those qualities in my speech. I found the picture of Nina, now permanently bent from the night I'd thought about ripping it up, and Liz made copies for me to give to the committee as part of my presentation.

Jules had asked her dad what he thought "See St. Francis from altar" meant, and he said that he had no idea. Nina had never said anything about St. Francis to him. So, after hashing it out, Liz and Jules and I decided that I would use this fifth item in my speech to discuss the mystery of what was ahead of me at Brown. I wrote about how embracing mystery was the hallmark of a great education, because mystery is what leads us to seek out knowledge.

Every day, Liz or Jules or both of them listened as I practiced my presentation. They applauded, gave me feedback, or gave me thumbs down if something seemed over the top. I put the whole speech on index cards. The afternoon before I left, Liz told me that I needed to memorize it. The index cards were distracting.

"She's right," Jules said. "It's going to be, like, perfect if you don't have to look at your cards."

I nodded in agreement. "Should I sing the song, or is that too much?"

"I say, sing it," Liz said with passion. "Sing it with all your heart!"

"Sing just a verse," Jules said, considering. "You sound really good. But I could also see it, like, getting awkward?"

"Perhaps she's right," Liz said. "Perhaps Crown Jules actually has a point."

"All right, it's settled," I said. "I'll sing the first verse only.

And I'll memorize these"—I waved my index cards in the air—"by tomorrow."

"You have the ferry ride," Liz said.

"And the bus ride," Jules added.

"You're going to do well," Liz said.

"You're going to kick ass," Jules said.

"They're going to love it," Liz said.

"They're going to, like, readmit you so fast you'll already be a sophomore," Jules said.

"That makes no sense," Liz said.

"She knows what I mean," Jules said with a shrug.

"Yeah, I do," I said, pausing for a moment to observe the scene before me: Jules sprawled on my sofa bed, rubbing the silky part of the blanket, and Liz with her legs crossed, one foot bouncing, one hand twirling a curl. They were my two best friends, and they would be for a long time.

"Thank you so much for everything," I said.

"Don't get sentimental on us till you're back in," Liz said.

"Well, in that case . . ." I said, as I threw my index cards in the air, took a running start, jumped on the sofa, and tackled them both.

"You're heavier than you look, mate!" Liz said.

Forty

I HEARD DAD'S TAXICAB WHISTLE FROM THE SIDELINES AS I
sprinted to catch a pass from a midfielder named Bitsy, who
was anything but. She had to be over six feet tall and her
legs looked so strong that they seemed like they could only
belong to a professional athlete. Or a man. I caught the pass,
which was so powerful it nearly pinned me to the field. But
I found my balance, rolled past a defender who looked like
she had issued from the same Norse god as Bitsy, and passed
to Fiona, a left attack wing so fast I swear her cleats were
smoking.

Even though my lungs ached and a cramp pinched my
side and it looked like Fiona was going to score all on her
own, I sprinted wide for a pass. My legs were shaking and

my heart was beating so fast it was in danger of exploding, but I was afraid if I stopped moving I just might drop dead on the field of St. Timothy's at the final scrimmage for the Women's Lacrosse Ivy League Training Camp.

I'd played lacrosse since the fifth grade, but the girls at this camp were of a different breed. Usually, I was the fastest girl on the field. I knew a couple of players in our high school league as fast as I was: Patricia Cassell, Katie Rothwell, and maybe, *maybe* Izzy what's-her-face from Middletown Academy. But this was a whole field of Patricias, Katies, and Izzys.

And not only were they all fast, they were also driven, well-spoken, and smart. They were in such good shape they could practically fly. They were focused, agile, alert; perfect pictures of health; excellence made physical. There wasn't a mediocre or even second-best among them. And all together, despite different hair color, skin color, and body shapes, in a weird way, they looked exactly alike. They looked like the finest examples of everyone I had grown up with. They looked like what I had always imagined I would become if I tried my hardest.

"Lacrosse is our life," Fiona said when we were stretching out before the scrimmage. She was a junior at Brown, originally from Virginia. "Three hours a day. Every day. And every weekend, too. It's awesome." As I stretched out my calves, my mouth went dry.

"Are you okay?" she asked.

"Yeah, I'm fine." I smiled. I didn't know how much these girls knew about my situation.

"You look like you just saw a ghost."

"Just nervous," I said.

"Don't be," she said, and smiled. "You're going to be great. Besides, you're already on the team."

When Fiona saw that I was open, she called out a play we'd gone over at halftime. I had never moved so fast or been so aggressive. I sprang free from the defensive wing who was guarding me, taking full advantage of a pick set by Bitsy, leapt up to catch the ball, and slammed it straight into the goal. The whistle blew. My team cheered. Two minutes later, I did it again.

It wasn't my stickwork, which was actually weak compared to the other girls', or my conditioning, which was below par and had me bent over and heaving after I'd scored. And it sure wasn't that I was more innately talented than the other girls. It was determination, that superpower that can be willed into existence by those with something on the line. It made me better than I should have been. It made me shine. Or maybe it was just that the other girls were playing a game, and I was fighting for everything I'd lost.

Whatever it was, it worked. I saw Coach Stacy smiling on the sidelines. She wrote something on her clipboard. At the end of the scrimmage, when the Brown kids were huddled up, drinking water and trading stories about the summer, she squeezed my shoulder and said, "Great job, Cricket." The assistant coach winked at me. Fiona gave me her number and told me I could call her if I had any questions or just wanted to hang out with the team in the next few days.

"Oh, thanks," I said. "But I'm going to be on Nantucket."

"You go to Nantucket? I love Nantucket! Do you belong to the Wampanoag?"

"I work there," I said. "I'm a waitress at Breezes."

"Cool," she said. "Call me when you're back in town."

"Holy crap," Dad said, when we got in the car. "You were like a fish leaping out of the ocean. You were like some kind of flying squirrel. Let me see those cleats. Are there springs in there?"

"I was fighting for my life," I said as I eased off my cleats and peeled away my socks. My feet were bright red and throbbing. A ruptured blister on my heel was oozing.

"You know what? You weren't a fish or a squirrel. You were a warrior!" He couldn't wipe the grin off his face. His forehead wrinkled with amazement. "I'm the father of a warrior. 'That's my girl,' I said when you scored that goal. 'That's *my* girl!'"

"Yeah. I did all right."

"You did better than all right. I'm proud of you, sweetie," Dad said; he kissed my sweaty hand. "I couldn't be prouder."

"That's what you said at my graduation party."

"I'm prouder now," he said, as we passed the white clapboard dorms of St. Timothy's and the idyllic, pristine Newport coastline came into view. "No matter what happens tomorrow. I'm as proud of you right now as I have ever been."

Dad and I went to the Newport Creamery. Dad drank a decaf coffee and watched in amazement as I ate a grilled-cheese sandwich and drank a whole vanilla Awful Awful, the Newport Creamery's signature milk shake, in about three minutes. I kept telling myself to slow down, but the shake was so cold and so sweet. If forgiveness had a taste, I thought as I wiped my mouth with my grass-stained hand, it would be this.

Forty-one

"YOU ASKED ME TO COME HERE AND EXPLAIN MYSELF, AND I thank you for the opportunity," I said; and I took a deep breath and made eye contact with each member of the committee in the small, formal room in the Brown Admissions Office. Claudia Gonzales looked even younger than she'd sounded on the phone. Coach Stacy was barely recognizable in a suit. Dr. Fantini, a tall, bow-tied dean from the science department, was the third member.

My hands were shaking, so I clasped them behind my back. I was wearing an outfit that Mom had ironed: a khaki skirt, a white blouse, and navy flats. Mom had blown out my hair and pulled it back with a silver barrette, just as she had done for picture day at Rosewood every year since I could remember.

Whatever anger and frustration she'd demonstrated when I first told her what had happened had morphed into mothering.

After she picked me up from the bus station, she'd made me my favorite dinner—spaghetti with clam sauce—put clean sheets on my bed, and even stocked the fridge with my favorite kind of yogurt. And that night, when I couldn't sleep despite being exhausted, she came into my room with her guitar.

"Oh, the summertime has come and the leaves are sweetly blooming," Mom sang softly. *"And the wild mountain thyme grows around the purple heather."*

"Will you go?" we whisper-sang together. *"Lassie, will you go?"*

"Remember when I used to sing that to you?" she asked. "Every night, you wanted to hear that song."

"Keep singing," I said. "And then sing it again."

And she did—we did, until I fell asleep.

The air-conditioning in the admissions office wasn't working. The four of us were perspiring. I took a sip of water from a bottle they had handed me when I walked in. As I fumbled to replace the cap on the bottle, it fell to the floor. Despite the fact that their eyes followed it to the edge of the carpet where it landed, I didn't dare pick it up for fear I'd spill the whole bottle, knock over the table, send a lamp crashing down, and set the building on fire. I placed the water bottle carefully down and continued.

"I want to start by saying that I know what I did was wrong. I know that I abused alcohol. I take full responsibility for my behavior, which was immature, cavalier, and potentially dangerous. It was the first time in my life getting drunk, and because of the repercussions, I take alcohol use very seriously." I took a breath and another sip of water. "It says in the Brown Code of Conduct that the university expects that members of the Brown community be truthful and forthright, so I've prepared as forthright and truthful an explanation as possible."

Coach Stacy leaned in. Dean Fantini recrossed his long legs. Claudia Gonzales sighed and made some notes. I pulled out the copies of the picture of Nina and the list and handed one to each of them. "This is Nina Clayton; she was in the class of 1989."

I went on to explain that she had been my best friend's mother and a role model to me. I told them that she had passed away the year before. I told them the story of the broken frame and my discovery of the list. Coach Stacy smiled as she read the list. "This is so eighties!" she said.

I held up the Rodin book. "Rodin said, 'Nothing is a waste of time if you use the experience wisely.' It was in the spirit of these words that I set about living this list on Nantucket. I wanted to do something with my summer besides serve lobster rolls to people in pink pants and seersucker jackets."

Dr. Fantini nodded.

"When I found this book in the thrift store, it felt like a sign so I began with number one: *Visit Rodin Museum in Paris.* I studied these pictures every night. I couldn't believe how alive they felt, even in a book that's thirty years old. The sculptures have the spark of life. When I watched a surfer out at Cisco Beach, I saw *Saint John the Baptist* and *The Walking Man.* I saw *The Thinker* and *The Kiss.* Because of Rodin, I saw something more than a surfer. I saw art in motion. So, in this first endeavor, I was successful. I had experienced Rodin without leaving Nantucket."

Dr. Fantini adjusted his glasses and made some notes.

"I moved on to number two: *Learn to drive and then drive Route 1 to Big Sur.*" I took a sip of water and continued. "I already know how to drive, so I decided to learn to drive stick. I learned in a 1976 Land Rover on the back roads of Nantucket." I smiled, remembering the day with Ben and how the car had taken off without us. "And this led me down a surprising path, both literal and figurative. I saw parts of the island I wouldn't have seen, but also I think learning a new skill can open up a new road. While I was focusing on driving, I allowed myself to sing without self-consciousness, and it reminded me how much I like to sing, even if I don't have perfect pitch. In pushing ourselves to try new things, we find other parts of ourselves, the back roads of our souls." I scanned the faces of the committee members. Coach Stacy and Dr. Fantini looked pleased, but Claudia Gonzales remained expressionless. Maybe I'd pushed it too far with "back roads of our souls." In a last-minute decision, I decided not to sing. Jules had been right. It was too awkward.

"When you look at number three, you might see the connection between the list and why I'm standing here today. *Drink Campari on the Amalfi Coast with Alison.* Alison was Nina's best friend. Nina's daughter, Jules, was my best friend. Until Nina died. The tragedy of her death separated us, and I missed her so much. Losing a best friend is like losing a piece of yourself, and I wanted so much to connect with her again. I wanted the ease we used to have in our friendship, an ease that seemed epitomized by the idea of drinking Campari in Italy.

"I was so inexperienced with alcohol. Like I said, I'd never been drunk before. That night, I was totally caught up with a feeling of freedom. At some point, I let that freedom get the better of me. I lost control. It was so scary." My voice shook a little. "I never want to lose control like that again. If anything good came out of this, it's that I have a deeper commitment to my own health and safety and that of those around me."

I mentioned that Jules had revealed to me that the Woody Allen movie Nina had been in was *Crimes and Misdemeanors,* and this made all of them laugh, even Claudia Gonzales. I told them that I had written a letter to Woody Allen to see if he would let me audition for him.

"How did that go?" Ms. Gonzales asked, blinking in amazement.

"Let's put it this way," I said, "I'm not exactly a working actress." They laughed again.

"I'm not auditioning for Woody Allen," I said, "I'm auditioning for the role of Brown student, and I am ready to throw myself into the part. See, I don't just want to read about Rodin in a book. I want to take a class with an expert. And I don't just want to look at pictures from the 1950s. I want to study midcentury America. Instead of drinking Campari from a liquor store on Nantucket, I want to take Italian classes. And while I'm pretty sure I don't want to audition for a movie, I want to know why people are so crazy about Woody Allen, maybe through a film-theory class.

"I know I made a mistake," I continued. "A big mistake. But I am exactly the kind of student you want. With this list, I've demonstrated that I live my curiosity. I pursue learning with a passion. I take meaningful risks. And I want to take more of them, here, at Brown."

"What about the last item on the list?" Ms. Gonzales asked, holding up her copy.

"Oh, yeah." I'd gotten so swept up in my grand finale that I'd forgotten about Nina's last wish: *See St. Francis from altar.* "That one's a mystery to me," I said, trying to remember what I'd planned to say. "It represents what I don't know, and maybe what none of us knows, what eludes us but keeps us looking."

"Wow," Coach Stacy said, beaming. "Good answer. "

"That was quite a presentation," Dr. Fantini said.

"We'll talk and get back to you in twenty-four hours," Claudia Gonzales said. Coach Stacy smiled and gave me a secret thumbs-up.

I nodded. "I look forward to hearing from you." Why, I wondered, did I feel a knot in the back of my throat? I thanked them all again and gathered my things. *This is what I want,* I told myself.

"You know, Cricket," Dr. Fantini said as I was leaving, "I think that last thing on the list is about Larsen's Comet."

"What do you mean?" I asked. "Why?"

"A group of French monks near the Italian border viewed this comet during the feast of Saint Francis and thought it was a sign from the heavens. There was a sickness in their village, and after the comet appeared, many were healed. They thought it was Saint Francis himself. Scientists have always credited the discovery of the comet to the Danish astronomer Anders Larsen. But some folks from a certain part of France have always believed it was Saint Francis. Was Nina French?"

"Her grandmother was," I said.

Dr. Fantini beamed. "The last time the comet was visible was in 1939, so her grandmother probably saw it herself, and perhaps she wanted her granddaughter to see Saint Francis in the sky. It's one theory, anyway. I can't explain the 'altar' part, though."

"I can," I said. "It's a place on Nantucket."

"Would it be a good place to see the stars?"

"It would be perfect," I said, realizing that if I could see the comet from Altar Rock, it would be the only thing on the list I could actually complete, for now, anyway. It was the one thing that Nina hadn't actually been able to do.

"This is the last week that the comet is going to be visible, and the forecast calls for rain for the rest of the week, so I suggest you get out there. It's not coming this way for another seventy-five years," Dean Fantini said. "I can't wait to tell my wife. She will love this story. It's very romantic."

"Wow, thanks," I said. "You solved the mystery."

"There's still plenty of mystery out there. For all of us," he said.

I thanked him, and as soon as I was out of the office, I pulled up the ferry schedule on my phone.

Forty-two

"JULES, I FIGURED IT OUT," I SAID, STANDING OUTSIDE THE
Brown admissions office. "You're not going to believe this.
But you know that last thing on the list? Your mom was
talking about Larsen's Comet. I guess a lot of French people
think that it was Saint Francis, appearing in a miracle. And
your great-grandmother is French, right?"

"Yes. She's French, all right. Why do you think I suf-
fered through so many years of Madame Smith? That's so
crazy. And you know what? Mom always said that Altar
Rock was the best place to see the stars."

"This is one thing on her life list that she didn't get to
do, Jules! We need to get out to Altar Rock tonight, because
it's supposed to rain the rest of the week and then it's not
coming again for another seventy-five years. Seventy-five

years! Oh my god, there's a fast ferry that leaves at six p.m. Can you get to Hyannis? Can you pick me up on the way?"

"Cricket, this is so cool, but I'm not going back to Nantucket. I'm with Jay."

Oh, I thought. Oh, yeah. She was in love, and when a person is in love, there is no one else as important as *that person*. I knew what that felt like. Once, I had felt that way. Once, Zack had been *that person* and I had been *that person* to Zack. I squinted against the pain of knowing that that wasn't true anymore.

"I just got here," Jules said. "Besides, I've already seen the comet. This list? It's your thing. Your thing with my mom. You go ahead."

"Are you sure?"

"Yeah," she said. "He did it last night, by the way. Dad's engaged."

"Really? I'm sorry."

"I'll get over it," she said. "We'll talk about it later, okay? Jay and I are at a restaurant. He's waiting for me. I kind of have to go."

"Okay," I said, starting my walk back home.

"But wait," she said. "How'd it go with Brown?"

"It went well," I said, heading toward Thayer Street. "I think I did it. I mean, fingers crossed."

"How was the scrimmage?"

"I scored. Twice."

"That's awesome! I knew it! Okay, Jay is waving to me.

He got us a table. Igottagoloveyoubye." I felt her growing up, arcing away from high school. I didn't want her to grow up any faster than I did. Now that we were best friends again, I wanted us to be in lockstep with each other, but she was getting out of Providence, even if only to Boston, and I had just fought with all of my might to stay.

As I walked down Thayer Street toward my mom's house, my heart was heavy. I was in the center of the Brown campus. And I knew every café. I knew every store. I knew every crack in the sidewalk. There was the Avon, the single-screen movie theater where I'd seen foreign films with Jules. There was the Thai place that Mom ordered from twice a week the year of the divorce. There was the hot-dog stand I'd been going to since I was six. I knew these streets so well I could've walked home blindfolded.

A girl in a Brown Women's Lacrosse T-shirt came out of the 7-Eleven and started walking in my direction. I saw Fiona and Bitsy a few steps behind her, chatting and laughing. I darted into the vintage clothing store where Jules and I had bought our Halloween costumes two years ago. I held my breath and watched them pass by from the window. Fiona's words haunted me. *Lacrosse is our life. Three hours a day. Every day. And every weekend, too.*

My phone rang. It was a Brown number.

"Hello?" I said. The bell above the door rang faintly as I left the store. I leaned against the glass of the storefront and pressed the phone to my ear.

"Hi, Cricket. It's Claudia Gonzales. I'm so delighted to welcome you back into the class of 2018. We were right about you the first time."

"Thank you," I said. "Thank you so much."

She went on to tell me about registration and orientation, but I could barely hear her. I was light-headed. My ears were buzzing. I felt faint. I sat on the curb. As soon as I hung up, I burst into tears.

Forty-three

I FELT ZACK BEFORE I SAW HIM. I APPROACHED ALTAR ROCK and shivered, even though the evening air was soft and warm and beckoning. I'd taken the bus and the fast ferry and then ridden one of the inn's bikes to Altar Road. I ditched it when I realized it'd be easier to walk on the wide dirt path. I felt Zack here, but when I climbed to the top of Altar Rock and saw him waiting for me, I lost my breath with surprise.

"No," I said. "You need to go. Because I'm not leaving until I see this comet, and we can't both be here."

"There's room for two," he said, fanning out his arms.

"Zack, come on."

"I needed to see you." He shifted his weight. "Jules called me. She told me that you'd be here. Because of Mom."

"You could've warned me. Is Parker here? Is your *girl-friend* here?" I covered my face and shook my head. "I came all the way from Providence. Please, Zack. Don't ruin this for me. Just go away."

"She's not here. And she's not my girlfriend. Look, if I told you I was going to be here, you would've run away." He stepped toward me. I stepped back. "Jules told me that you got back in?"

"Yeah," I said, "after fighting like a warrior." Zack smiled, and I felt a flash of embarrassment at my word choice. "But what Parker did? It's not okay. It will never be okay. And the fact that you didn't break up with her, that will never be okay with me, either. Ever."

"I did break up with her. This morning. There's a lot you don't know about her."

"Don't ask me to have sympathy for her, Zack. Jesus Christ. Don't do that."

"She tried to kill herself this year."

"Oh." I covered my mouth.

"You can't just break up with a girl like that. You have to make sure she's stable. I mean, can you imagine what it would be like if she tried it again, right after I broke up with her? If she'd actually done it? I'd have to carry that my whole life."

"I'm sorry," I said quietly. "I had no idea."

"She's got a real problem," Zack said. "I tried to tell you without telling you. Jules did, too."

"Why didn't you just tell me?"

"When a United States senator asks you to keep your mouth shut"—he shook his head—"you keep your mouth shut."

"But I still don't understand why. Why does she care about me?"

"She saw the video I took of you," he said, "and it was so clear."

"What was?" I wanted more than suggestion from him. I wanted him to spell out his thoughts for me in plain, brave English. No more high fives. No more drunken almost-kisses. No more meaningful underwater touches. I crossed my arms. "What was clear?"

"That I'm still in love with you!" He sounded almost pissed off about it.

"Oh." The words I'd dreamed about and hungered for didn't come out the way I would have expected. I stood there, stunned, trying to absorb them.

"She shouldn't have tried to sabotage you," he said. "It was really messed-up. She's really messed-up. But it's not so simple. She was there for me last year. I was all alone. My mom died. I was at a new school. I was lost."

The idea of Zack alone, in pain, felt like a pill stuck in my throat or a splinter on the verge of infection, too tender to touch. "Why didn't you tell me?" I asked. "I was lost, too. I was alone."

"I tried to tell you," he said. "That call before Thanksgiving?"

"You interpreted that all wrong. I told you."

"Parker actually showed up, in person." My blood pressure dropped below sea level. "Everything changed. I had friends. I had fun. And one night it just kind of happened. I didn't know what I was getting into. I didn't know how screwed up she was. I don't think she did, either. The doctor said depression can come on suddenly at this age."

"This is a lot to deal with. Do you have any idea what the past few weeks have been like for me?"

"I'm sorry. I'm so, so sorry," he said. He wrapped his hand around mine. I closed my eyes. It was *his* hand. Zack's hand. *That person's* hand. "I understand if you don't feel the same."

"I do, though. I do feel the same."

He took my other hand and leaned in so that our heads touched. "I've missed you. That night. I wanted to be with you. I wanted to kiss you so badly." He stepped closer so that our cheeks were touching, so that he was whispering in my ear. "I wanted to do more. I wanted to do everything."

He turned to kiss me. I kissed him back, but pulled away when I felt tears rising. "This whole thing really hurt, Zack. I think we need to just be friends for a little while." I said this even as my whole body was sending me another message. He met my gaze and nodded. "I'm so confused. About so many things."

"Tell me," he said. We sat on the rock and he put his arms around me. I looked up. The sky was getting darker now, but it was also getting cloudier. "Tell me what you're confused about."

"I don't want to go to Brown." I leaned into him.

"What?"

"I've lived in Providence my whole life. I want to live somewhere else." It felt so good to release the truth, to surrender to it. "I don't want to go. And I love lacrosse. But I also feel, I don't know, done with it."

"When did this happen?" he asked, weaving his fingers with mine.

"It's been happening," I said, wiping away tears with the heel of my hand. "All summer." I tried to pinpoint the moment when I had started to want something else; to go somewhere else; to be myself, but different.

"Because of that guy?"

"No, not really." Was it that night singing on the beach? "I don't know." Was it when I first cracked open the Rodin book? Or was it that moment on the ferry, when I'd seen Nina's list and felt her with me?

"You don't have to go to Brown," Zack said, pulling me close.

"People will think I'm crazy. I mean, after all this." I pulled my knees to my chest and lowered my head. "It's not like I have a plan. It's not like I know what I'd even do."

"You'll figure it out. You're the smartest person I know."

"Me?"

"You."

"Oh." I smiled into my arm. "Do you think we're going to see this comet?" I looked up, wishing the clouds would part. I thought of something that Ben had said that day we met on the ferry, about how the weather on Nantucket is often the opposite of what it is on the mainland. I probably would've been able to see the comet if I'd stayed in Providence. "I can't believe the one thing your mom didn't get to do on her list has been in front of me the whole time."

"Above you," Zack said. We lay back on the rock in silence for a while, waiting for the sky to clear up. Every minute, we inched closer until we were curled up together. When we were officially spooning, he pulled his arm away and sat up.

"What are you doing?" I asked.

"Trying to be friends."

"Don't try *that* hard." We laughed as he lay back down and I rested my head on his chest, an ear to his thumping heart. "I need some time, okay?"

Maybe Ben had actually been on to something. Maybe there are times when labels like *boyfriend* and *girlfriend* and *friend* just don't apply. Maybe what couldn't be named was just as real as what could be. Maybe sometimes love existed in the spaces in between. Maybe, I thought staring up at the clouds, I just need to let what wants to be revealed appear.

Forty-four

I DIDN'T SEE LARSEN'S COMET UNTIL A WEEK LATER.

This was after I'd called Brown and asked to defer my acceptance for a year, after I'd broken the news to my family that I needed what Liz called a gap year. It was after Liz and I decided that we would move to New York together and get an apartment, maybe on the Upper West Side, or maybe in Brooklyn. It was after Jules and Jay had started at BU together and Zack had returned to Hanover, and the only people left on Nantucket were the late-season tourists and the people who worked there.

I called George Gust and explained why I would make the perfect assistant. I was organized, passionate, and perspicacious (SAT word). He hired me on the spot. Liz was going to find work in a hotel, maybe go to school for social work. We both agreed she was good in a crisis. She and I decided to stay on Nantucket through early September. She had to wait for Gavin to get back from Bali, and I could make as much money as possible before we moved. I was close to having ten thousand dollars in the bank, which was enough to get me on my feet in New York. Rosemary and Jim were still going to match what I made, but instead of giving it to me right away, they would put it in a bank account for a year where it couldn't be touched and would gather interest.

I saw Larsen's Comet when I was walking home from Breezes. I looked up and saw a smudge of light in the moonless sky. It was carelessly bright, naturally captivating, effortlessly stunning. Just like Nina. I had no idea how I'd missed it all summer.

I texted Jules and Zack: Look up!

Jules texted back: St. Francis in the sky!

Zack joined in: Awesome.

I wrote: True beauty!

A second later, as I was standing with my head tilted all the way back, Zack texted me privately. It was a picture of me the night at Something Natural, looking at the camera, looking at Zack, my eyes wide open, awake with wonder, my smile a little mysterious. Beneath it he wrote: True beauty.

Later, back at the inn, I opened the journal Mom gave me. I finally knew what to do with it. I picked up a pen, wrote *Cricket's Life List*, and started to dream.

Epilogue

LIZ AND I MOVED TO NEW YORK IN THE MIDDLE OF September. We found a little apartment in Park Slope, right near George Gust's. It's a fourth-floor walk-up with one tiny bedroom, but the windows are big, the water pressure is great, and as former chambermaids, we keep it extremely clean. My dad drove us down in the minivan. We bought a pair of twin beds from 1-800-Get-A-Bed and a kitchen table and chairs that we carried twelve blocks all by ourselves from someone on Craigslist. When we smelled bread baking on our way home, we had to stop for a snack. We bought warm, fresh brioche rolls with butter and jam. We couldn't wait, so we ate them seated at our new table, right on the sidewalk.

Liz is taking a social work class at NYU and working at

the front desk of the Soho Grand Hotel, where people go crazy for her accent. "They think I'm so posh and proper!" she says with giddy delight. "If only they knew I'm a humble Yorkshire lass, with knickers from Target and a ravenous appetite for love."

I started working for George right away. I organize his office, keep track of his research, run errands, maintain his calendar, and talk things out with him when he gets stuck or wants a fresh perspective. No two days are ever alike, and I love that. I've talked to Hillary Clinton's personal assistant twice on the phone, which is cool any way you look at it. George always has a cup of coffee waiting for me when I show up, and I make sure he has a salad for lunch at least twice a week.

George really only needs a part-time assistant, so I picked up a couple of waitressing shifts at a neighborhood bistro around the corner from our apartment. It's called Vanessa Jane's. The walls are painted red and covered with black-and-white photographs of Paris. The onion soup is perfect on a crisp fall day, the coq au vin melts on the tongue, and the crème brûlée is heaven in a ramekin. The owner, the actual Vanessa Jane, is more like a friend than a boss. I don't make as much as I did at Breezes, but it's a lot less stressful, and I can always cover for someone if I need a little extra cash to buy a sweater or a dress that I have to have.

Sometimes, when I see pictures of Jules hanging out in her dorm with a whole group of new friends, I wonder if I made the right decision, but then I remind myself that

I still have my spot at Brown waiting for me. George told me that Columbia has an excellent journalism program, so I'm applying there as well. "There's nothing wrong with options," George said, and I think he's right.

I ran into Amy/Amelia on the N train last week. I almost didn't recognize her in her suit and loafers, but when I called her name, she came right over and sat next to me. She'd moved back to New York when she was hired at a high-profile law firm in midtown. She said Ben stayed on Nantucket, which I figured he would. "But I had to move on," she said. "I'm a city girl." I gave her my number and told her to call me sometime, but I have a feeling that's not going to happen.

Zack and I are doing what we swore we never would: long distance. Only, we're doing it the old-fashioned way, with letters. We write to each other at least once a week. It gives me the space and time to get to know him all over again after our year apart. When I see the white envelopes with my name and address scrawled in his boyish hand-writing in our dented mailbox, I rush up all four flights of stairs in seconds flat. The letters inside, written on paper torn from a notebook, are long and full of funny details. He writes exactly like he talks. I write back right away with my tales of Brooklyn, George, the customers at the restaurant, and the people I see on the subway. I'm collecting his letters in a yellow and blue Cuban cigar box I found at an antique store. We're writing a story together. Our story. When he asked me in his last letter to spend Thanksgiving with him on Nantucket, I wasn't about to make the same mistake I did last year. I sent a postcard right away from the Brooklyn Botanic Garden that said simply, "Yes."

I can't stop smiling as the ferry slows, approaching the now familiar shore. It's a different season now, and the sun washes the island in amber light. Instead of lush green, the tree-tops are red, yellow, orange, and brown. The late November breeze is cold off the choppy water, but I'm too excited to feel a chill. I throw my duffel bag over my shoulder and search the dock for Zack. I see him and hold my breath. He's wearing his black peacoat and a red scarf. I can't wait to show him my new haircut. I can't wait to be with him in winter, to snuggle next to him under a blanket on the porch and trade stories and kisses. I can't wait to hold him. He sees me and his face fills with light. As I walk down the ramp, my heart heats to life. It's a spark, a flame. A fire.

Acknowledgments

I'D LIKE TO THANK: EMILY MEEHAN, MY AWESOME EDITOR. Sara Crowe, my dream agent. The whole team at Disney Hyperion, especially Laura Schreiber, Jamie Baker, Elizabeth Holcomb, Monica Mayper, and Marci Senders. Vanessa Cross Napolitano and Kayla Cagan, my steadfast writing group members, for their insight, honesty, kindness and humor. Maryhope Rutherford for her sensitive reading of the first draft. Eileen McGrath, Jennie Haas, Maggie Moran, Bob Crowe, the Nantucket Police Department and all the wonderful people on Nantucket who welcomed me, patiently answered my questions, drew me maps and provided the kind of details that fire up a writer's mind. Sharon Gardner for our invaluable conversations about the psychology of these characters. My family and friends, especially my parents. And Jonny, whose storytelling talent, imagination, and wild sense of humor are only a few of the reasons why I am so lucky.